THE WICKED WOLFE

A BLACKHAVEN BRIDES NOVELLA
DE WOLFE PACK CONNECTED WORLD

MARY LANCASTER

DE WOLFE PACK: THE SERIES

By Aileen Fish
The Duke She Left Behind

By Alexa Aston
Rise of de Wolfe

By Amanda Mariel
Love's Legacy

By Anna Markland
Hungry Like de Wolfe

By Autumn Sands
Reflection of Love

By Barbara Devlin
Lone Wolfe: Heirs of Titus De Wolfe Book 1
The Big Bad De Wolfe: Heirs of Titus De Wolfe Book 2
Tall, Dark & De Wolfe: Heirs of Titus De Wolfe Book 3

By Cathy MacRae
The Saint

By Christy English
Dragon Fire

By Danelle Harmon
Heart of the Sea Wolfe

By Hildie McQueen
The Duke's Fiery Bride

By Kathryn Le Veque
River's End

By Lana Williams
Trusting the Wolfe

By Laura Landon
A Voice on the Wind

By Leigh Lee
Of Dreams and Desire

By Mairi Norris
Brabanter's Rose

By Marlee Meyers
The Fall of the Black Wolf

By Mary Lancaster
Vienna Wolfe
The Wicked Wolfe

By Meara Platt
Nobody's Angel
Kiss an Angel
Bhrodi's Angel

By Mia Pride
The Lone Wolf's Lass

By Michele Lang
An Honest Woman

By Ruth Kaufman
My Enemy, My Love

By Sarah Hegger
Bad Wolfe on the Rise

By Scarlett Cole
Together Again

By Victoria Vane
Breton Wolfe Book 1
Ivar the Red Book 2
The Bastard of Brittany Book 3

By Violetta Rand
Never Cry de Wolfe

CHAPTER ONE

T HE BOYS JUMPED out of the cart almost before Linnet could draw the pony to a halt. Their feet crunched over the dirty, frost-hardened snow of what might have been a yard or a terrace.

Bolton, the family mastiff, bounded after the boy.

While they raced each other toward the gloomy old house, Linnet exchanged humorous glances with her little sister.

Laura's gaze quickly moved to the building. "Is it really haunted?" she asked.

Although not yet dusk, the January afternoon was bleak and gray, adding to the overall eeriness of the deserted house. It was not large by country house standards, though bigger and more substantial than the local cottages.

"Of course, it is not haunted." Linnet threw off the blanket and moved to the back of the cart to step down. "I'm only humoring the boys bringing them here, but I fear they are doomed to disappointment. Besides," she added as Bolton began to bark, "I don't fancy any ghost's chances against *him*."

Laura laughed and jumped down after her. While she closed the door and ran to join her brothers, Linnet hung a nosebag on the bored pony and patted hm. As she strolled after the others, the boys peered in the dirty ground-floor windows. Bolton paced up and down the length of the building, snarling to himself. The whole scene possessed a bizarrely gothic charm that appealed to Linnet.

"What's the matter with Bolton?" William demanded.

"He senses the supernatural," Henry said with sepulchral glee.

Linnet laid a calming hand on the dog's great head. "More likely he smells the vagrants who have passed by doing exactly what you are doing."

"Vagrants?" Henry repeated. "Do you suppose they got into the house?"

"No," Linnet replied, "for there's no obvious damage to the door or the windows."

"If there's anything in there, I can't see it," William said, scowling with dissatisfaction. "The windows are too filthy."

"Well, nobody has lived here for decades," Linnet pointed out, peering over his shoulder in vain.

"Who does it belong to?" Laura asked.

"Some minor scion of the Wolfe family," Linnet said. "According to Mrs. Grant, the vicar's wife. But they're so rolling in wealth, they seem to have forgotten about their little cottage up here. It was rented for a time, but no one bothers with it anymore. So naturally, all the local children scare each other with tales of hauntings."

"Well, Bolton doesn't like it," Henry said, hurrying after the dog to the front door.

Bolton barked, jumping up to push the door with his front feet. This made him taller than Henry, who grinned and pushed him down, though only to try the latch.

The door creaked open.

Before anyone could express even surprise, Bolton bounded over the threshold, snarling.

"Grab him!" Linnet exclaimed. "Bolton, come *here*!"

Bolton paid no attention to her or to the children who were all shouting at him to halt, sit, or come this instant. In fact, with all of them chasing after him, he may well have thought it a game—or a hunt, for he was clearly following some inflaming scent. Which did not bode well. Since the door was not locked, it seemed more than likely someone was in here, whether servant or vagrant, and Bolton did not like anyone except his own family. She doubted he would draw blood unless provoked, but by his sheer, staggering size, he was terrifying to the majority of sane people.

Bolton thundered through the entrance hall and down the main passage, knocking over a small table on his way. Linnet did not take the time to pick it up again, merely charged after him. He jumped up on his hind legs and crashed through a door on the right.

An unworldly screeching rent the air, chilling Linnet's blood. Pushing the suddenly frozen Henry aside, she ran into the room and slid to a halt.

In the room's gloomy light, a pair of wide, wild eyes stared right at her from the back of a sofa. Or no, they were staring rather at Bolton who snarled and growled right in front of her. With a screech, the eyes seemed to leap upward. In fact, a whole, grotesquely human little figure flew through the air and seized onto the chandelier hanging from the ceiling. Bolton jumped, trying to catch it.

"It's a devil!" Laura cried in terror. "Linnet, run!"

At that moment, the chandelier came away from the ceiling and the creature fell, screeching even more loudly. It landed on the sofa amid a hail of unlit candles and glass beads. Bolton lunged just as Linnet hurled herself on the dog, and a previously unnoticed figure loomed up from the sofa.

Candles and glass tumbled from him, and the creature clung to his neck.

"What the devil?" said the thick voice of a man as he clutched his head with one hand and the human-like creature with the other.

Linnet, with both her arms around Bolton's neck and her fingers gripping his collar, made a discovery. "It's a monkey!"

The man on the sofa regarded it. "So it is. The monkey, I remember. You, I do not. Nor the dog. Is it a dog? Or a pony?" He frowned. "And children! I most certainly don't recall you. Where the devil did I find you all?"

"I'm afraid you didn't, sir," Linnet said apologetically, for the man did not speak like a vagrant or even a servant. Her best guess was a steward or some kind of man of business, though he seemed a very odd one. "We stumbled upon you when our dog ran into the house. I think he smelled your monkey."

The man wrinkled his nose. "I'm not surprised. He's rank. I'll put it down to fear of the beast you call a dog,"

Bolton, apparently confused by the conversation, had subsided somewhat. No longer straining against Linnet, he concerned himself with glowering at man and monkey and uttering occasional low-voiced growls whenever either of them moved.

"Well, if you wouldn't mind shaking hands with me," Linnet suggested, "he will probably accept *you*. Though I'm less sure of the monkey. Laura."

Obediently, Laura slid into place in front of Bolton, wrapping her arms around his great neck while Linnet sat up. The boys took their places on either side of him, each grasping his collar.

The man on the sofa, a large and rumpled looking young gentleman with his blond hair standing up in uneven spikes, watched these maneuvers with interest. His lips twitched as Linnet knelt facing him and held out her hand.

"How do you do, sir? I am Linnet James, and these

are my siblings, Henry, Laura, and William. The beast is Bolton."

"I am very pleased to make your acquaintance," the man replied gravely, taking her hand. His felt cold, the skin a little rough, but his grip was firm and civilly brief. "Especially, Mr. Bolton's."

Laura and William giggled.

"Maybe the monkey should shake hands, too?" Henry suggested, grinning.

"Of course he should. Napoleon, bow to the ladies and gentlemen."

"Napoleon?" William grinned. "You called your monkey Napoleon?"

"Well, no, the sailors I found him with called him that," the man replied, watching critically as the monkey warily separated himself and made a short, elegant bow with his "hand" over his heart.

"How delightful he is," Linnet said warmly. "Will he bite if I offer my hand?"

"No, he's only a baby and quite tame."

In fact, the monkey put its little paw in Linnet's and chattered when she smiled at it, stretching its lips at her. Next, it warily held out its paw to Bolton, who stepped back out of reach.

The monkey clung to its owner once more. The man then surprised everyone by holding his own hand out to the dog. The James family held its collective breath while Bolton deigned to step forward again and sniff the human fingers.

"Oh, well done, sir," Henry approved. "It's the only way to make friends with him but most people are too frightened."

"I like animals," their new friend informed them.

"Where did you get the monkey, sir?" William asked eagerly. "Is he from Africa?"

"No, the sailors found him in Gibraltar when his mother died, but unfortunately, some of their shipmates were too rough with him, so I took him off their hands."

"You should take him to all the fashionable events in Blackhaven," Laura said with glee. "The skating party, the assembly room ball!"

"He does not do well at balls, sadly."

"You mean you have taken him to one already?" Linnet asked with undisguised admiration.

"Not exactly. I left him in his cage in a cloakroom because I had no time to go home first. I don't know how he got out—I suspect some mischievous soul released him. Anyway, he spent a long time swinging from Countess Lieven's curtains." He glanced at the ceiling. "She had a chandelier, too, a much larger and finer one than that."

The children chortled.

"I'm sorry we upset poor Napoleon," Linnet said with contrition. "For he has made quite a mess."

"I expect you brought him here because there is no one to mind the mess," Laura guessed.

"Not exactly," the man admitted. "I came to sell the place. I suppose I'll need to get someone in to repair the ceiling."

"Ah, you are the Wolfes' man of business," Linnet said, pleased with her first guess, although it struck her almost immediately that men of business, even those who acted for such mighty families as the Wolfes, probably didn't get invited to Countess Lieven's balls.

"Not exactly," the man said again, his erratic gaze coming back to rest on her. He rubbed his forehead. "You're very beautiful," he observed, "and your family is charming, even Mr. Bolton. But if you'll excuse the questions of a poor creature struggling with the most monumental of self-inflicted headaches…er…what are you doing here?" He cast a quick glance at the filthy window. "It can't be much after dawn."

Linnet blinked. "It's three o'clock in the afternoon."

His eyes widened. "Well, I'll be…" He frowned. "Well, that explains the headache."

"You need a hair of the dog," Linnet said sympathetically.

The man smiled, a somewhat devastating smile that must have dropped women at his feet in droves. Linnet was glad not to be so impressionable, though even she acknowledged a pleasant little tingle.

"Are young ladies meant to know of such low matters?" he inquired.

"Probably not," Linnet acknowledged. "But our brother Laurence seemed to need them a lot."

"I trust he has outgrown such uncivilized behavior—as indeed, should I."

Linnet said nothing, for the wound was still raw.

"He might have," William said doubtfully. "But he died a year ago in the Pyrenees."

The amiable stranger's eyes flew to William and then back to her. "I'm sorry. What regiment was he with?"

"The 95th, the Rifle Brigade."

"An excellent body of men," he said. "You must be

very proud."

Unable to speak, Linnet merely swallowed and nodded.

"Are you a soldier?" Henry asked with interest.

"I was." He brushed all the detritus off his lap. "I sold out after Toulouse. Please don't think I am not grateful for the attention, but—er—why are you all here?"

"We came to prove the house was not haunted," William said, twisting his motivation just a little. In truth, they came to see the ghosts. "And your Napoleon scared the wits out of us because he looked just like a demon, until our eyes got used to the gloom."

"Who says the house is haunted?" the man asked, rising and stretching prodigiously while the monkey dangled from his neck by one arm.

From Linnet's still kneeling position, he seemed very tall and lean. His clothes were as rumpled as the rest of him, but then he was in his shirt sleeves. He wore no cravat and his coat, which had been covering him as he slept, had fallen on the floor when he first sat up.

"The boys in Blackhaven told us it was," Laura said scathingly. "And so, we had to come out here to see for ourselves."

Their host bent and picked up his coat, shrugging into it with the apparent ease of a man not used to the services of a valet.

"It has proven a rather more exciting expedition than I expected," Linnet admitted. "And I'm very sorry we barged in on you."

"Don't be," he said at once, stretching his hand down to her. "I'm not."

Blinking, Linnet took the proffered hand, and with his aid, rose to her feet. She felt a blush rise to her cheeks. "You are very kind and understanding," she murmured. "And now, we must go. Bolton!"

Bolton, who had been sniffing around the room, lifted his great head and trotted over to her at once.

"Back to Blackhaven?" their host asked.

"Yes. We have taken a house there for a month, while my mother tries a course of the waters for her health."

"Ah." Their host strode across to the window and rubbed at the filthy pane with his elbow. "The dirt's on both sides," he said, irritated, "but from what I can glimpse of the daylight, it will be gone before you get back to town."

"We have a lantern," Linnet said. "Besides which, the pony knows the road and is so slow he could not cause an accident if he tried."

"One pony for all of you? I'm not surprised he's slow."

"I'm not sure that's complimentary," Linnet observed and won another of his devastating smiles.

"I meant the dog, of course."

"Oh, he runs most of the way," Henry said carelessly. "Unless he decides there is a threat, he's usually very obedient and doesn't chase sheep or cattle. We only put him in the cart when we reach civilization, so people aren't frightened by him."

"Very wise," said their host, offering Bolton his hand once more. The dog sniffed it in more friendly fashion this time and allowed the man to stroke his head. He glanced at Linnet. "I have no food in the house to offer, but I can give you tea before we start out? Then I'll bring my own lantern and escort you to Blackhaven."

"Oh no, we could not trouble you," Linnet said at once, ignoring the disappointed glares of her brothers.

"No trouble," said their host. "I need to find that hair of the dog." He swung the monkey back up onto his shoulder and made for the door. "But tea first, once I deposit Napoleon in his cage."

"Can I come?" William asked eagerly.

"Of course."

Henry went with William in the end, while Linnet and Laura cleared a space on the sofa and sat down.

"I like him," Laura observed in a low voice. "But who *is* he? He doesn't seem like any man of business who ever comes to *our* house."

"I don't think he is," Linnet said, allowing in the inescapable conclusion at last. "I think he's the owner, one of the Wolfe family."

CHAPTER TWO

"A WOLFE STAYING here without servants?" Laura said doubtfully. "Besides, he said he was a soldier."

"There have been great soldiers in the Wolfe family since medieval days," Linnet argued. "Though I suspect such an unimportant property as this has passed through younger sons to our host."

The boys were back surprisingly quickly. William held the door open for Henry, who carried the tea tray, and their host strolled in behind. Both boys spoke at once, telling her about the fabulous cage the monkey had in the back garden with a little tree and a bath, and how their new friend was an expert in making tea.

"He learned in the army," William said, clearly awed.

"From watching my men brew it for me," their host said deprecatingly. "And now from watching me, you may make it for your mother and sisters."

Henry laughed at the very idea, but William frowned. "It might yet come to that," he said ruefully, "if we can't pay Hetty's—"

"Shall I pour?" Linnet interrupted hastily.

"Please," their host said, taking Laura's vacated place on the sofa while the children sat together on the floor opposite, with Bolton stretched out behind them.

"What is your name, sir?" Laura asked bluntly.

"Wolfe," he replied, accepting the cup and saucer from Linnet.

"Not *Colonel* Wolfe?" Henry exclaimed, awed.

Their present Wolfe grinned. "Lord, no. He's a distant cousin. I was a lowly captain."

"That's not lowly," William said stoutly. "Laurence was only a coronet. Why are you going to sell the house? Don't you like it?"

Captain Wolfe wrinkled his nose. "Do you?"

"It has good proportions," Linnet observed. "It is a nice shape, and I do like the stone carving above the door and windows."

Wolfe blinked. "I haven't noticed those."

"They need a good clean."

"Like the rest of the house. I was hoping for a quick sale but I suspect there's too much work to be done first."

"Why do you want to sell it quickly?" William asked.

"Will!" Linnet admonished. "That's none of our business."

"Oh, I don't mind, since we're friends," Wolfe said easily. "I need the money."

"For more monkeys?" William asked hopefully.

Wolfe laughed. "What a good idea. But no, just to pay some debts. Perhaps I shall have some left for monkeys.

Watching him drink his tea, it crossed Linnet's mind that despite his good natured and easy-going exterior, there was some profound sadness in him that went way beyond the headache of overindulgence he admitted to. His gaze moved, catching hers, and the question she almost asked him—if there was something wrong that they could help with—died in her throat. Instead, she blushed to have been caught staring.

She finished her tea and set it down on the nearby table. "The china is pretty, too," she babbled. "The house must have many selling points." She regarded the fine cornice work in the ceiling. "If I were you, I would repair it and clean it and redecorate, and then see if I wanted to live in it."

He blinked, clearly startled by the suggestion. "Live in it?"

"Well, one must live *somewhere*, and Blackhaven is a pleasant town."

"My ancestors were borderers," he observed, "back in the dim and distant past when all one needed to do to for wealth was beat up the right set of rebels or invaders."

"Cheer up," Linnet said lightly. "At least you got to beat up the French."

His eyes laughed, though again with that fascinating hint of hidden sadness. "So I did."

"We should go," Linnet said reluctantly. "Drink up boys and girls!"

Wolfe swallowed the last of his tea and set down his cup. "Give me a few minutes to saddle my horse and I'll meet you at the front."

Dusk had fallen when they left the house and the temperature had dropped considerably. Linnet hoped the road would not be too slippery. She removed the pony's nose bag, which was almost empty, and bade the children get out the blankets while she lit the lantern.

"He's had a good rest," she said optimistically, patting the pony's neck. "And will go like the wind."

The children were still laughing at this when their host appeared, mounted on a huge, beautiful black horse.

"I say, sir!" Henry exclaimed in excitement. "Is he a cavalry horse?"

"He was. Carried me through many a wild day." Wolfe bent from the saddle, handing Henry his lantern. "That should give us enough light. The clouds are clearing, too, so we should get decent moonlight. Let me lead the way, and hopefully your old pony will follow Nosey here."

Despite the growing darkness, the return journey was considerably quicker than the outward. With Bolton bounding along beside them, the pony roused himself to a decent trot to keep up with the other horse. The road glistened with frost, as did the piles of cleared snow on either side, and some of the ruts were frozen hard enough to rattle Linnet's bones when they drove over them. But in all, it was a surprisingly pleasant ride. Although she did not feel the need of Captain Wolfe's escort, there was something curiously exciting about having him there in front of her. He rode as if the horse was part of him. She could easily imagine him spending days in the saddle at a time, eating, fighting, even sleeping there.

The town of Blackhaven was already in sight, and Bolton summoned into the cart, when two men suddenly erupted from the wood ahead, brandishing pistols and shouting.

"Highwaymen!" William breathed, awed.

"Don't be silly," Linnet said at once, although her stomach twisted with fear because it seemed William was right. The men were running between the cart and Mr. Wolfe, who at that point was several yards ahead, investigating the state of the road. The pistols were pointing at her.

And in case she was still in any doubt, one grabbed at the pony's bridle while his friend commanded, "Stand and deliver!"

The pony came to a halt without her instruction. Laura clutched at Linnet's arm in fright, although the boys seemed more excited than frightened. Bolton, roused from his post-run slumber, stood up and growled.

The footpads eyed him with some alarm, their eyes

wide in the lantern light.

"Deliver what?" Linnet demanded. Although furious, she could not risk one of them shooting her siblings. Or poor Bolton. Ahead, she could no longer even see Wolfe. She hoped he was galloping into town for help. "We have no money or anything of value."

This seemed to throw the footpads, who scowled. "Coins, gewgaws, silk, jewels…"

"My brother has a well-used linen handkerchief. Otherwise, there are only blankets and the clothes on our backs!" As soon as she spoke the contemptuous words, she prayed she had not simply given them fresh ideas.

"Hand over the wiper," growled one, walking around to the side of the cart to receive Henry's handkerchief.

Bolton, growling deep in his throat, began to snarl, lunging his great head over the side of the cart, his teeth gnashing.

Laura threw her arms around the dog's neck. "Don't shoot him!" she begged.

The footpad snatched back his outstretched hand, eyeing Bolton with understandable wariness.

"Don't you have horses?" William asked the ruffian. "Wouldn't it be more exciting if you were riding? Then you could catch something more lucrative than a governess cart."

"Less of your lip," the footpad muttered, snatching the unappealing "wiper", which Henry obligingly leaned out of the cart to hand over.

Beyond him, at the edge of the trees near the side of the road, stood a large, riderless horse which definitely had not been there the last time Linnet had glanced that way. And it looked very like Wolfe's. In which case, where was he?

"Hurry up, for God's sake," uttered the man holding the pony. Both the footpads glanced up the road toward the town, as though expecting further traffic, or perhaps the law. And in fact, surely Linnet could hear galloping hoofbeats?

"What else you got there?" demanded the other, stashing the handkerchief in his pocket. "We'll take the large blanket. At least it's useful."

Resentfully, Linnet began to gather up the biggest blanket which had been covering the boys. As she moved to the edge of the cart, she glimpsed the top of a blond head, and then the cart door swung open.

"Bolton!" Wolfe's voice called, and the dog tore free

of Laura's grip and bounded out of the cart.

Snarling, Bolton launched himself at the nearest footpad, who went down under his weight with a scream. By then, Wolfe had run the length of the cart and the pony. As the footpad there began to rush to his comrade's aid, Wolfe grabbed him by the shoulder and hit him square in the jaw. As he stumbled, Wolfe grabbed the pistol from his hold and ran on to where Bolton stood on top of his victim, his huge jaws threatening the ruffian's neck. Wolfe picked up his fallen pistol, too.

His recovery of the situation had taken only seconds. Linnet laughed with as much relief as delight. "Oh, well done, sir!" she exclaimed, dropping the blanket and clapping her hands.

"Not as well as you might think," Wolfe said. He was examining the pistols, although his head jerked up suddenly. "Who is this? Not another of them?"

Henry groaned. "Lord, Linnet, it's your knight of the pen."

To Linnet's astonishment, the newcomer was indeed Sir Constantine Fotheringham, who, for some reason, had taken such a shine to her that he wrote vast quantities of dubious poetry to her. The boys thought it hilarious, and had dubbed him her knight of the pen, though in truth, they found his company somewhat wearing.

He galloped furiously up the road to them, brandishing a pistol Linnet hadn't known he owned, and yelling, "Be gone, villains!"

The footpad Wolfe had laid out, scrambled to his feet and legged it. His friend whimpered under Bolton's slavering jaws.

"Good boy, Bolton, leave him to me now," Wolfe recommended.

Bolton obliged, which drew a quick breath of laughter from Wolfe before he hauled the miscreant to his feet and extracted Henry's handkerchief from his pocket.

"You're too late," William informed Sir Constantine impatiently. "So, you might as well put the gun away. Captain Wolfe has already dealt with them."

"But we're very grateful for your efforts," Linnet said hastily, for she did not wish to be unkind. "It was most brave of you. Only what on earth are you doing out here?"

"I was simply seeking my muse in the stars on this beauteous night," Sir Constantine said, almost mechanically for him, for his wary gaze was divided between the prisoner and Bolton who, for some reason, never took to the poet. "And although I deeply regret the plight in which I find you, I am honored to have had the privilege of playing some small part in your salvation."

"What part was that?" William asked Henry, without troubling to lower his voice.

"Allow me to introduce Captain Wolfe," Linnet said hastily.

The retired soldier pocketed both pistols and strolled up to offer his hand to Sir Constantine, who remained mounted. "No longer Captain," he said casually. "I sold out. I'm Jack Wolfe. How do you do?"

"Sir Constantine Fotheringham," Linnet murmured.

Sir Constantine barely troubled to reach down to Wolfe's outstretched hand, allowing the merest touch of two fingers. "Your servant, sir," he said distantly. "And how is it you come to be here at the right moment? Were you also just passing by?"

"Oh no, I'm escorting Miss James and her family back to Blackhaven."

"It seems you've made but a poor job of it," Sir

Constantine observed.

Wolfe merely smiled, although the children made outraged noises and Linnet said sternly, "I will not have that, sir. Captain—*Mr.* Wolfe dealt with the matter most efficiently and at great personal risk."

"Oh, great risk," Wolfe murmured in a deprecating tone. Behind him, his prisoner took advantage of his distraction to edge away. Wolfe turned. "Go on then, run for it," he advised, and gave him a boot in the behind to help him on his way.

The man ran like a hare. Bolton allowed him a glance before returning to more important matters, which seemed to be growling at Sir Constantine, who kept a nervous eye upon him.

"You're letting the varmint go?" Sir Constantine demanded in clear astonishment.

"Well, he'd only slow us up and everyone is too cold," Wolfe said carelessly. "Shall we press on?"

"Bolton!" Linnet called hastily, and the dog reluctantly left off staring at Sir Constantine to jump back into the cart. Wolfe closed the door and whistled for his horse, who trotted up as if this was a common occurrence.

"Does he do that in battle, too?" Henry asked eagerly.

"I don't think he'd hear me in battle," Wolfe said. "In any case, I always tried my hardest to stay on his back." He mounted with light, easy movements and trotted forward as Linnet, again, gathered up the reins and urged the pony into motion.

But Sir Constantine did not like that arrangement. "Why don't you guard the rear?" he suggested loftily. "And *I* shall lead the way."

Wolfe regarded him. Linnet wondered if he would obey. After all, the command was somewhat insolent considering who had overpowered the footpads.

Wolfe shrugged. "If you wish. I'd go a bit faster, though, or everyone will freeze to death. The pony will keep up with you." He drew his horse aside and let the cart draw by before he rode along beside it.

"Who the devil is *he*?" he asked the boys, nodding to the front of their little cavalcade.

"Linnet's admirer," Henry said with a grin in his voice. "He's mad as a cake and utterly tiresome, besides writing the most nauseating verse you're ever likely to come across."

"There's no need to be unkind," Linnet admonished, although his behavior since his arrival on the scene of their hold-up was hardly appealing.

"Marry him, then," Henry dared her.

"I have no intention of marrying anyone," Linnet said with dignity.

"Why ever not?" Wolfe asked.

"I prefer to live with my family, rude and obnoxious, though some of them are."

Henry grinned. "You don't mean me, do you?"

"How could I possibly?" Linnet asked sweetly. She glanced at their savior. "Thank you for what you did. I was so afraid they would shoot the children."

"There was no danger of that," Wolfe assured her.

She frowned. "You needn't be so modest. There were two pistols trained on us!"

"They weren't loaded," Wolfe said mildly.

Linnet's eyes widened. "Not… *Why* not?"

He shrugged. "To frighten without the possibility of killing, I suppose. Or perhaps they ran out of ammunition."

She searched his face, handsome and yet shadowed in the glow of the lantern. "Did you know this when you attacked them?"

"I suspected—something in the way they waved the pistols around. They looked too light. Anyway, I had enough doubt to make it worth the risk. With apologies to Mr. Bolton who was not consulted."

Bolton thumped his tail. Linnet glanced at the straight road ahead. The pony was happily following Sir Constantine's mount. "And even if they fired at you, we would still have had time to get away before they could reload."

"You are a master tactician," he said flippantly.

"You had no need to take such a risk for us," she said low. "But I thank you with all my heart."

"No need," he replied. "It's the most fun I've had since I came home. And at last we are in Blackhaven. I suppose your knight knows your direction?"

"Oh, he knows," William muttered. "You're not thinking of leaving us here, are you, sir?"

Linnet knew a silly moment of panic, no doubt associated with the fright they had just had. Though there was little danger in the well-lit town at five o'clock in the afternoon.

"In the circumstances," Wolfe said, "I believe I shall see you to your door."

"You must come in and be introduced to Mama," Laura said with enthusiasm. "She loves to meet new people and she doesn't get out much just now."

Although Linnet was intent on guiding the pony through traffic, she felt his gaze, imagined it warm like a caress and chided herself for idiotish fantasies more akin to Sir Constantine's than her own down-to-earth view of people.

"Of course you must," she managed. "If we are not intruding on your time."

"My time could not be better spent."

They turned into Shore Place, where Sir Constantine dismounted just beyond their front door. By the time Linnet guided the pony in behind him, Brewster was hobbling down the front steps.

"There you are!" he scolded. "You said you'd be back before dark."

"Sorry, Brewster," Linnet said, throwing him the reins while the children and Bolton exploded out of the cart and into the house.

Wolfe dismounted in time to hand Linnet out of the cart, while Sir Constantine scowled in annoyance from the saddle.

"There is nowhere to tie up the horses," he intoned. "So we shall be on our way."

"Nosey will wait," Wolfe said cheerfully.

"Goodbye, Sir Constantine," Linnet said civilly.

"Thank you for your escort and your brave interven-
tion."

While Brewster took her place in the cart to drive it
round to the mews behind the house, she ran blithely
up the steps and into the house, very aware of Mr.
Wolfe following and the odd sense of excitement that
seemed to accompany him.

CHAPTER THREE

NOT FOR THE first time that day, Jack Wolfe wondered what the devil he was doing. He had been on a bit of a spree in Blackhaven last night and got home sometime after four-in-the-morning. However, the cold air having freshened him up on the journey, he'd continued to drink himself into unconsciousness. In fact, when he'd wakened, he knew very well he was still drunk. The sight of several children and a slobberingly vicious dog trying to eat Napoleon had almost sobered him up, but it was the sheer, laughing beauty of the accompanying lady that enchanted him.

A middle-aged maid took his coat and hat with a disapproving glare which he could hardly grudge her, for in a befuddled kind of way, he was pursuing Miss James, and not with honorable intentions. However, as the clouds of alcohol began to clear out of his pounding head, he realized that what he had taken for discreet demi-monde was in fact, shabby gentility.

This new perception was reinforced when he walked into the rented house's fading drawing room and was introduced to Mrs. James, who looked just as sick as the children had said but welcomed him with a genuine smile.

"Mr. Wolfe," Linnet murmured. "Who has been most forbearing and kind."

Had he? Somewhat startled by this explanation of his behavior, he took the lady's frail hand and bowed over it.

"I suppose it was that animal," she said with resignation. Bolton, clearly recognizing the description, lifted his head from his paws and thumped his tail on the floor.

"He broke into Mr. Wolfe's house and we had to follow him," Laura said, "in case he took a dislike to anyone."

"Which he did," William added. "But we caught him quickly after that."

"I am relieved to hear it," Mrs. James said wryly. "I can only apologize, sir, for my wayward family!"

"There is no need," he assured her. "They are, rather, your *delightful* family."

"You are most kind. Now, remind me which Wolfe you are?"

"John Wolfe,'"

"Hmm, are you the Earl of Warrenton's cousin?" she said, scrutinizing him. "Or, perhaps Lord Ottley's son?"

"Ottley's son," he admitted, and felt Linnet's gaze on his face with something very like disappointment. "Are you acquainted with my parents?"

"Your mother and I came out in the same year, but no, I'm afraid I cannot claim acquaintance. Linnet, is Hetty bringing tea?"

"Not for me," Wolfe said. "I'm afraid I have to go."

"Of course!" Laura exclaimed. "You have still not had your hair—"

"Haircut," Linnet finished hastily.

"Indeed?" said Mrs. James. "I have heard the barber in High Street is very good."

"Thank you, ma'am," Wolfe said gravely, "then that is where I shall go. May I call again?"

"Of course, you are most welcome. We visit the pump room most days, but are generally home in the afternoons."

"Then I look forward to seeing you again." He

bowed to her and winked at the children who all grinned back at him.

"I'll show you out," Linnet said, "since Hetty will be making tea."

He held the door for her and let her lead him back downstairs.

"I'm afraid we are rather short of servants," she said apologetically.

"But that was not always so?"

"Since my father's death, largely. Everything was a bit of a mess, but we shall come about, if only Mama can get well,"

"Is she seeing a reputable physician?"

"Our physician at home advised her to come to Blackhaven for the waters, and gave us the name of a Dr. Bellamy who has recently set up his practice here. He seems very knowledgeable and obliging."

Wolfe nodded. By then they had reached the front door, and he offered his hand with a rather rueful smile. "Goodbye, Miss James. You and your family have been a breath of fresh air in my thick head."

She gave him her hand, and her eyes laughed back at him, catching his breath. "I think I may safely say that is the most *natural* compliment I have ever received."

"Mine are all natural," he said. "For I never say what I don't mean." He released her hand to lift his hat and coat from the stand by the door. With a last glance at her, he opened the door and went out, closing it again behind him.

Nosey greeted him with a whinny and he mounted, trotting away without a backward glance. It made no difference. Her face remained in front of him, laughing and full of fun, and yet entirely innocent. She shone like a beacon, bright, caring, and clever.

And beautiful …

Wolfe gave himself a metaphorical shake. He was not given to sudden passions and romantic fantasies. Not that he didn't like women, for he did, a lot, but his first care had always been for the army and his duty. It was the loss of this life that was making him soft. Well, that and the fog of last night's excesses.

As he made his meandering way toward the tavern where he'd spent a good deal of last night, he passed a rather pretty church. Rumor said an old army friend who'd sold out several years ago had settled as a very unlikely vicar in Cumberland. For some reason, Wolfe had it in his head that his church was in Blackhaven.

He reined Nosey in.

Set farther back from the road was a decent-sized detached house, probably the vicarage. There were lights in several of the curtained windows and he contemplated calling in. Then the distant cry of a baby drifted over to him from the house, reminding him that Grant—if this was Grant's home—was probably married now. And Wolfe must look thoroughly disreputable, without his necktie or even a clean shirt. He probably stank of stale brandy. Hell and the devil confound him, had he really called on Mrs. James in this state?

With a faint groan that was half-laughter, he turned his attention back to the church. There was a light in there, too. On impulse, Wolfe dismounted, wound the rein around the railing in case Nosey followed him down the path, and walked up to the church door.

A few candles lit at the front of the church showed him a man in neat clothing standing by the front pew while he gathered up a collection of papers and books.

Straightening, he glanced in Wolfe's direction. "Good evening."

It was definitely Tristram Grant, although he looked odd without his military uniform.

"Good evening," Wolfe returned, strolling forward.

A faint frown tugged at Grant's brow as he peered toward him. In the dark part of the church, Wolfe wouldn't be so recognizable.

"I'm looking for the vicar," Wolfe added. "At least I am if his name is Grant." He emerged into the candlelight and Grant's eyes widened.

A breath of laughter shook his old captain. Grant thrust out his hand. "Mad Jack Wolfe, as I live and breathe! What the devil are you doing here?"

"Language, vicar," Wolfe mocked, gripping the offered hand and searching the familiar face. Grant had not aged much. But a new serenity had replaced the turbulence in his eyes. "You look well."

"I am well." His gaze swept over Wolfe. "Unlike you. Looking a trifle rough, Jack."

"I am," Wolfe said carelessly. "Self-inflicted and easily cured."

Grant grinned. "You haven't changed. Come up to the house and tell me everything."

"Not really fit for it right now," Wolfe said, spreading open his coat to reveal his lack of tie and general state of rumpledness. "Did I hear a baby crying? Yours?"

"My daughter," Grant said proudly.

"Then there is a wife."

"There is," Grant agreed, flushing slightly. "Come and be introduced. Kate does not stand on ceremony, and you will most certainly be invited to dinner."

"Not today," Wolfe said gruffly. "I'd rather not disgrace myself or you. But I will come tomorrow, if I may, now that I've tracked you down."

"By all means," Grant said at once. "We'll be at home most of the day." He began to douse the candles, and picked up the last one to light their way to the door. "When did you arrive in Blackhaven? More to the point, why?"

"Got a small property just to the west of the town. Thought I might sell it."

"Really? Which property?"

"Haughleigh House."

Grant paused with one hand on the door. "That's yours?"

"For now."

"Must be in a bit of a state."

"Oh, it is. I doubt I'll make the quick sale I aimed at, but at least I got to run into you."

Grant let the door fall shut behind them and

glanced at him. There might have been concern in his eyes. "We have a comfortable spare room and the baby doesn't cry much."

Wolfe laughed. "She would if she saw me. So would your wife. "Until tomorrow." He stuck out his hand again.

Grant shook it. "Tomorrow," he agreed.

Wolfe strode away toward Nosey.

"Jack?" Grant called after him. "Where are you going?"

"The tavern, of course," said Wolfe.

≫≫≫≪≪≪

ALTHOUGH THE TAVERN was where he had spent a good deal of last night, having gone on there from the hotel with a few like-minded acquaintances, his memory of it was quite hazy. He couldn't remember it being quite so dirty and smelly, though he did retain the overall impression of rough shadiness.

After a first dark and suspicious glance, the other patrons ignored him. In fact, one in the corner huddled further into his coat as though trying to vanish entirely. Wolfe strolled up to the bar and ordered his hair of the dog. For a rough seamen's tavern, it served excellent brandy. Vaguely, he wondered how the new peace with France would affect smuggling operations. Probably not hugely, since smuggling was as old as import duty.

With his grubby glass full of brandy, he turned to face the room. The gaze of the man disappearing into his coat slid away. Wolfe regarded him thoughtfully. There was a redness to the man's cheek that ran down into the upturned collar of his shabby coat. It could easily be the footpad he'd struck.

Testing his theory, he sauntered over to the man's table and pulled up a stool. The alarm in the ruffian's eyes was unmistakable before he looked deliberately the other way. Even then, looking ferocious, he twitched in his seat as though he wanted to be any-where in the world but here.

"I think I have something of yours," Wolfe re-marked.

"Doubt it," the man muttered.

Wolfe took one of the confiscated pistols from his pocket and laid it on the table. The man snatched at it, his eyes darting, although in the true spirit of the place, no one paid him a blind bit of attention. Wolfe was quicker, slamming his hand over the footpad's and pinning it to the table, with the pistol beneath.

"If you want it back, you have to answer a few questions. Otherwise, I give it to the magistrate."

The man's eyes widened in outrage. In this establishment, it was probably bad form even to acknowledge the existence of magistrates. "What do you want?" he muttered.

"Why did you hold up a shabby governess cart full of children? Did you expect rich pickings?"

The man shrugged. "Take what we can get."

"You'd have had more luck holding me up a few yards in front. Or the man who came riding up the road only a couple of minutes later."

"Ah, well he was armed."

"I wasn't."

"Didn't do you any harm, though, did it?" the man retorted bitterly. He snatched up his ale with his free hand and Wolfe glimpsed the tattoos on his fingers.

"You're a sailor," he observed.

"Ship's in dock."

"And you have family to feed," Wolfe guessed. "So, when someone paid you to hold up a particular vehicle, only to run away as soon as he appeared, you jumped at it. Easy work."

"And no one'd have got harmed if you hadn't stuck

your nose in." The man sniffed. "If your guess was true."

Wolfe searched the defiant face and made a decision. "If you accept any other such work, I'll break both your arms before I haul you off to the magistrate and you'll hang. If he asks you again, send to me and I'll pay you whatever he offered. He isn't a man who ever risked a finger for his country."

"Soldier?" asked the sailor, and Wolfe nodded for the sake of simplicity. "I thought so. All right."

Taking this for assent, Wolfe lifted his hand and watched the pistol vanish into the sailor's pocket. "I'm only doing this because the pistol wasn't loaded. Was that your idea or his?"

"His. He didn't want the lady hurt, even by accident. Or so he said." The sailor sniffed. "It's my belief he didn't want it going off anywhere near *him*."

"I expect you're right." Wolfe knocked back his brandy. "You'll make sure your friend knows the deal, too?"

"If I see him."

Wolfe stood, nodded to his new friend, and walked out of the tavern. His bed, with its slightly musty sheets, was calling him.

⇒⇒⇒⟨⟨⟨

LINNET WOKE THE following morning with the tingle of excitement in her veins. Because she had met Mr. Wolfe, because he might call, and she would so like to have him as a friend. Quite why, she didn't know, but she sensed a kind of affinity between them that was both comfortable and thrilling. She had been short of friends, recently.

Having washed and dressed, she went to her mother's room, where Hetty was serving her mistress breakfast in bed and coaxing her to eat.

"Good morning!" Linnet said cheerfully and sat on the edge of the bed from where she could kiss her mother and allow Hetty to fasten up the back of her clothing. It was something of a morning ritual. "Your toast looks good, Mama."

"You eat it, dear."

"I'd love to, but I'd better breakfast with the children. Besides, you need to eat it or you won't have the energy to walk round to the pump room."

Only to please her, Linnet knew, her mother nibbled at the edge of her toast. Linnet stayed, chatting inconsequentially until one piece of toast was entirely gone.

"Now another," she said cheerfully, and left her to Hetty's ministrations while she roused the children.

Since her siblings tended to cause havoc in the pump room—especially the day William had brought Bolton inside—they were generally left with Hetty while she and her mother went there alone. The children's task was to take Bolton for a short walk on the leash. Henry was just about strong enough to hold him now if he lunged, but in truth, the mastiff tended to be well behaved and obedient with the children, growling only when strangers had the temerity to speak to them.

Eventually their mother came downstairs dressed for her outing, and Linnet picked up her old cloak from the hallstand while Brewster held open the door.

"Perhaps that pleasant young man will call today," her mother said as they made their slow way down the street. "Mr. John Wolfe."

"Perhaps," Linnet said calmly.

Her mother took a deep breath. "You must not hold back from marriage for my sake. Laura and Hetty will manage very well, and I would like to see you settled…" …*before I die.* The unspoken words hung between them like an eternal echo.

Linnet managed to laugh. "Peace, Mama, I met the man only yesterday, and I very much doubt he is hanging out for a wife!"

"Well, there is always Sir Constantine, who comes from a very good family, too, if not quite one of the Wolfe stature. He does talk a lot of fustian, of course, and I'm not sure his temperament is *precisely* suited to yours, but he is quite flatteringly taken with you."

"I have no idea why," Linnet remarked. "There are much prettier—and sillier—girls than I, who would listen in total enchantment to his poetic adulation."

"You have beauty and vivacity and intelligence," her mother said indignantly.

"Well, there's the thing," Linnet argued. "I suspect he actually prefers quiet, submissive girls who hang on his every word. The Lord alone knows what has drawn him to me."

"Linnet," her mother protested.

Linnet only laughed, glad to have turned the subject from John Wolfe.

As they sat in the pump room, her mother gamely sipping the water that at least tasted better than that of Bath, the vicar's wife came and sat by them with her own glass. She was hoping, apparently, to restore her energy quickly after giving birth to a daughter only a couple of weeks ago.

Mrs. Grant was not like any vicar's wife Linnet had ever met before. For one thing, she was young still and astonishingly beautiful and wore the loveliest gowns. On the other hand, she was not remotely vain and never quoted pious verse from the Bible. In fact, she was fun, and Linnet rather liked her.

"By the way," Mrs. Grant addressed Linnet. "I should not have advised you to go to Haughleigh House, for apparently the owner has appeared out of the blue and is staying there!"

"I know. We went yesterday and ran into him. Almost literally." Linnet told the story of Bolton and the monkey, and Mrs. Grant laughed till she clutched her abdomen.

"Oh, goodness, don't make me laugh so hard."

"Are you acquainted with Mr. Wolfe, then?" Linnet's mother inquired.

"Not personally, no, but my husband is an old friend. They served in the same regiment at one time. Apparently, he promised to call on us today, so I am agog to meet the man behind the legend of Mad Jack

Wolfe."

Intrigued, Linnet could not help asking, "What legend? Is that really how he's known?"

"Oh, only to his fellow officers, I'm sure. Due to his propensity for leading forlorn hopes, I believe. What did you think of him?"

Thrown by the directness of the question and the confusion of her own reactions to him, Linnet felt herself blushing and could do nothing to stop it. "That he is funny and kind and just a little sad."

"He did not seem sad to me," Linnet's mother intervened. "Just a whirlwind of activity. I mean, who gets their hair cut at half-past-five in the afternoon?"

Linnet swallowed down the sudden surge of laughter.

Mrs. Grant looked slightly confused, then, as Mrs. James returned the greeting of an acquaintance, she said quietly, "Tristram—my husband—thinks he is lost."

It's the most fun I've had since I came home. His words about fighting, capturing, and scaring off the footpads came back to Linnet, along with the indefinable sadness behind his laughing eyes. "Perhaps he is."

CHAPTER FOUR

H AVING SLEPT LIKE the dead for twelve hours, Wolfe woke feeling human again and washed his entire body with soap and cold water. Much refreshed, he dressed in clean clothes from his trunk and sallied forth to Blackhaven, where he finally obtained the haircut Linnet had wished upon him.

From the barber's, he strolled up to a pleasant looking coffee house and sat in the window watching the world go by. Despite the relaxing surroundings and the taste of decent coffee, his thoughts were not all cheerful. Was this all there was to be in his life now? Utter boredom punctuated by self-destructive sprees?

Well, yesterday hadn't been boring. It was that as much as his attraction to the fair Linnet that inclined him toward protecting the family. It was a bit of a come down from protecting his country and its fighting men, but a promise was a promise.

He finished his coffee and walked round to the

vicarage where he was shown immediately into the study.

There, he bent double in laughter at the sight of Grant at his desk, surrounded by books and papers, busily writing with a tiny baby resting in one arm.

"If you wake her, I will knock you out cold," Grant warned. "Better still, I'll let you walk her round the house while I finish my damned sermon."

"Damned sermon?" Wolfe mocked. "What kind of church do you run here? Let me see this little Grantette."

Grant sat back in his chair to give him a better view.

"She's tiny," Wolfe marveled. "Look at those perfect, miniature ears. She's prettier than you."

"She has her mother's looks."

"What's her name?"

"Nichola."

Wolfe couldn't help smiling at the baby, though he caught himself before it went on too long and threw himself into the armchair at the corner of the desk.

"Kate is out," Grant volunteered. "She goes to drink the waters to see if they make her less tired."

"Do they?"

"No, I think only sleep can do that. But it takes her out of the house and lets her talk of something other than babies. Talking of sleep, you look better than yesterday."

Wolfe grimaced. "I feel better than yesterday. Although it was an interesting day. Tell me, do you know a family called James? They don't live here, have just come for the waters. The mother is sick."

"I can't say I do," Grant replied apologetically.

"What about a would-be poet rejoicing in the name of Constantine Fotheringham?"

"Ah, yes, him I know."

"What do you know?"

"Man's a bit of an ass and has as much talent for poetry as my big toe, but he is enthusiastic and appears to be harmless."

Wolfe frowned and jumped up again. He strode to the window and back. "Would it surprise you to hear that he paid a couple of ruffians to pretend to hold up a cart full of children and a young lady? Just so he could appear the romantic hero who rescues them?"

"Yes," Grant admitted. "That would surprise me. Is it true?"

"I'm pretty sure it is. In his favor, he instructed said

ruffians not to use loaded guns, but damn it, Grant, you can't go around frightening people like that."

"No, you can't," Grant agreed. "He does seem a very…focused character. And now he is focused, perhaps obsessively, on winning this Miss James? Is he likely to succeed?"

The very idea of Linnet with Fotheringham was revolting. Wolfe gave a crooked smile. "I would doubt it. The children call him her knight of the pen and clearly dislike him."

"Perhaps he has other attractions. I believe he is quite wealthy, for example."

And the James family was quite clearly short of money. Wolfe's stomach twisted unpleasantly.

The baby stirred in Grant's arm, making tiny little noises.

"She's waking up," Grant observed. "I hope Kate won't be long."

Wolfe regarded the tiny creature with fascination. "It's an interesting road you travelled. From the Peninsula to…this. I have no idea why, but it seems to suit you."

Grant shrugged. "I am useful here. As I grew up, I found war too complicated for my conscience." He fixed Wolfe with his steady eyes, much as he had done when Wolfe was his lieutenant. "Did you find that, too?"

"I don't know. At the moment, I miss the army too much to judge."

"Then you *did* sell out? Why?"

Wolfe threw himself back into the chair. "If it matters, because I promised my father. He only bought me my first commission under duress, on the promise that as soon as France was beaten, I would come home."

"And here you are, where you have no wish to be."

Wolfe smiled. "I would like to be here for a visit."

"To sell Haughleigh House?"

"I wouldn't need to if I was in the army." He hesitated, then added, "I've been behaving badly, and my father, quite rightly, refuses to pay my debts or advance my allowance."

"You're selling it to pay gambling debts?"

"If you play, you have to pay. But no, if you want the truth, I've paid what I owe and now have nothing left which makes living damned difficult. *That's* why I need to sell." His lips twisted. "One has to pass the time."

"Going to the devil, Jack?" Grant asked casually.

"Oh, I'm pretty much there."

Perhaps fortunately, a faint commotion beyond the door distracted them. The baby's eyes sprang open a moment before the study door did, and a beautiful, raven-haired lady swept into the room.

"She isn't crying!" the lady exclaimed. "How wonderful. Tris, I have to—" She broke off, coming to a standstill as Wolfe rose to his feet.

"My old friend, Jack Wolfe," Grant said, standing and rocking the baby who had begun to wriggle and girn. "Jack, this is my wife, Kate."

"Oh, I have been hearing all about you!" Mrs. Grant exclaimed, offering her hand with easy friendliness. "How do you do."

Wolfe bowed over her hand. "Perfectly, now. I'm delighted to make your acquaintance, Mrs. Grant."

"And I yours," Kate assured him, withdrawing her hand to take the baby who was working herself up to a rage. "But you'll forgive me if I take this rude little baggage away and feed her? I hope you are staying for luncheon."

"Well," Wolfe observed, as the door closed behind her. "No wonder you are looking so pleased with yourself. Your wife is as charming as she is beautiful."

"I think so," Grant said complacently. "Then you will stay for luncheon? I want to hear everything."

BY THE TIME the gentlemen joined Mrs. Grant for luncheon, they had drunk a toast to their friends who were never coming home and then thrown off the somber mood in more amusing reminiscences. Wolfe, though more than happy to live in the past for a little longer, felt compelled by curiosity and civility, to discuss other subjects over luncheon.

Mrs. Grant proved a delightful hostess, her manner vivacious, although with odd moments of fashionable languidness that seemed to hang around her and add mystery. She was clever, witty, and clearly interested in him.

"Oh, I almost forgot," she exclaimed toward the end of the meal. "I have to apologize for blabbing about haunted houses in front of the James children, for I hear they disturbed your rest—and your monkey!—yesterday."

"Monkey?" Grant said, clearly intrigued.

Wolfe laughed. "I thought I was back in the war, only I couldn't understand why the French were bombarding us with candles. I was not at my best."

"And yet you fended off highwaymen single-handedly," Mrs. Grant observed.

Wolfe glanced at her. "Who told you that?"

"Miss James."

"My memory is hazy on that score," Wolfe lied. "I expect I was bored. In any case, the pistols were not loaded."

"You remember that much," Kate marveled.

"Modesty is wasted on my wife," Grant said. "She sees right through you."

"Thank you for looking after them," Kate said, "for I have come to like the family very much during our short encounters."

Wolfe regarded her thoughtfully. He was generally able to judge character quickly and accurately, and in Kate Grant's case, he had the further proof of her choice of husband.

"I, too," he said. "And their lack of protection worries me. Is Mrs. James very ill?"

"I believe so. But, you know, Linnet is very capable."

"I don't doubt it. But does she go out in society much?"

"No, for Mrs. James is not well enough to chaperone her to parties or the theater."

"Does she have no suitors other than Fotheringham?"

"Are you applying for the position?" Kate asked.

"Hardly," Wolfe said, his mind already moving on. "Dr…Bellamy, is it? Is he the best physician in the area?"

"No," Grant and Kate said at once.

Wolfe raised one eyebrow in amusement.

"We are biased," Kate said. "In favor of Dr. Lampton."

"Because he is your friend?" Wolfe asked.

"Yes," Kate admitted. "But, also, because he is an excellent physician. Bellamy flannels and flatters and is used now by many of the visitors who find him less…abrasive."

"Where can I find this Lampton?"

>>><<<

WOLFE MANAGED THE briefest of meetings on Dr. Lampton doorstep. The doctor proved to be both younger and brusquer than expected.

"Leave your name and direction with my housekeeper," Lampton commanded. "I have a broken leg and a birth to deal with, and I won't be back until late."

"Tomorrow will do," Wolfe said, only half-amused. "I'm asking for a friend, on the recommendation of Mr. and Mrs. Grant."

Lampton allowed him an extra glance over his shoulder. "Then leave your friend's name and direction."

Fortunately, the housekeeper was more helpful, and Wolfe did indeed leave Mrs. James' name and direction with her, along with his own for the doctor's bill. Then, before he called on the James family to warn them of the expected consultation, he tracked down the discreet but slightly shady pawnshop behind the high street.

When he opened the door, he discovered a lady before him. Arguing spiritedly with the pawnbroker, she did not at first notice him. But he knew her voice right away, and as he strolled up to the counter, she cast him an impatient glance that quickly turned into an expression of appalled shame.

"Mr. Wolfe," she whispered.

"Miss James."

CHAPTER FIVE

H ER GRANDMOTHER'S PEARLS really were the last thing of value the James family had to sell. They had been bequeathed to Linnet and she was loath to let them go. Eternally optimistic, she convinced herself their fortunes might miraculously recover, and resolved to pawn rather than sell them outright. At least she should obtain enough to pay Dr. Bellamy, although the size of his account had staggered her mother into deciding never to see him again.

Accordingly, leaving the children with Hetty while her mother retired for a nap, Linnet donned her ancient mourning hat with its useful veil, and slipped out to the pawnshop. She had discovered its existence only the day before yesterday from overhearing a conversation outside the pump room. Located behind the high street in what was little more than a narrow alley, both the shop and the neighborhood looked insalubrious in the extreme. She imagined hidden eyes watching her progress along the alley, and was only too aware of the few people lounging in doorways as she passed.

It was almost a relief to enter the pawnshop—and to discover it empty save for the smiling man behind the counter. She lifted her veil and approached him.

Linnet did not precisely know the value of the pearls, but she knew they were good. The pawnbroker's first offer dismayed her, and she immediately made to snatch them back off the counter.

He was faster. "Don't be hasty, Miss. I can see you are in need of a good price. Let me have a closer look and I'll see if there's any way I can make a better offer."

Linnet felt out of her depth here. When she had sold the previous pieces, it had been to the reputable jeweler used by her father in more fortunate times. Here, the atmosphere was sleazy, the broker somewhat greasy, and she had a bad feeling she was going to be "done". This feeling doubled when he increased his offer by a mere two pounds.

Despite arguing back with spirit, she knew she was going to have to let them go for his trivial sum. It was that or nothing, for she could not take the time or the money to go to Carlisle, let alone York.

"You'd get more if you sold 'em outright," the pawnbroker admitted. "But then they're gone forever. This way, you can always get them back."

A shadow fell over her and she glanced up, half-annoyed, half-afraid to be recognized in such an establishment.

It couldn't have been worse.

"Mr. Wolfe," she managed.

"Miss James." It was no consolation that he looked stunned.

More than that, with his jaw shaved and his hair cut, he looked both awe-inspiring, and more handsome than ever. He wore a well-fitting blue coat over a plain white waistcoat and smart pantaloons. His cravat was neat without being intricately folded. And his blue eyes bored into hers. "How may I be of service?"

"Oh, not at all," she said at once, blushing a fiery red. "My business is all but concluded."

"Return the lady's pearls," Wolfe snapped at the pawnbroker.

But Linnet was not having that. If she left now, she could never come back, and Dr. Bellamy's payment would be short. She tilted her chin. "There is no need." But she had no scruple about using him to increase the broker's offer. "But I do insist on a better offer, do I not?"

Wolfe's eyes narrowed, then lifted to the pawnbroker. "Indeed, you do. By twenty guineas at the very least."

"Sir!" the pawnbroker expostulated. "I cannot go higher than another five!"

"Twenty," Wolfe insisted, "or we both take our rather lucrative business elsewhere."

The struggle waged obviously across the pawnbroker's face before, with ill grace, he opened a drawer and counted out his original offer plus twenty guineas.

"Thank you," Linnet said, accepting the money and the laboriously written out ticket.

She was afraid to breathe, for although she hadn't obtained anything like the worth of the pearls, it was still enough to pay Dr, Bellamy, receive another consultation, and pay some household bills. It was not sustainable, of course, but they could go on for another few weeks, which would, hopefully, see an improvement on her mother's health.

She was at the shop door, with Mr. Wolfe reaching to open it for her, before she grasped that he meant to leave with her.

She stopped. "But you have not conducted your own business."

"I would rather conduct you away from here."

"But I cannot be seen with you. You are too...*notable* a person."

"I'll take you part of the way," he said. "If you prefer, I'll follow you,"

"That would be silly!" She considered, then sighed, and drew down the veil of her hat. "Then thank you again."

She could not deny her journey along the alley and the street beyond was more comfortable with his solid presence by her side. The loungers miraculously disappeared.

"You must think it very odd to discover me in such a place," she managed.

He shrugged. "I find it worrying. Of course, we all find ourselves in hard times occasionally, but have you no one to conduct such unpleasant business for you?"

"So that I won't be diddled?" she said ruefully.

"They exist to take advantage of your misfortune."

"And yours," she pointed out.

He inclined his head. "Mine is self-inflicted. Your own difficulty, I suspect, comes through circumstances beyond your control."

"I own I thought it would be less expensive in Blackhaven for a month," she confessed. "But it hasn't worked out that way. Still, once Mama is well again, then I may look for a position as a governess or some such and then we may be comfortable."

He blinked at that, as though unconvinced by her optimism. She didn't blame him.

"Has your mother's health improved in Blackhaven?" he inquired.

"A little, perhaps," Linnet replied with determined hope. "To be honest, I imagined the waters combined with a new treatment of Dr. Bellamy's would make much more difference. But Dr. Bellamy's treatment seems to be very much like our own physician's. And now Mama has taken him in dislike and won't see him again." She did not mention the size of his bill as the main reason for her mother's dislike.

Wolfe only nodded. "You know Mrs. Grant, I believe."

"Oh yes. We like her immensely."

"She mentioned another doctor in the town whom she highly recommends. A Dr. Lampton. He won't charge for an initial consultation. If you like, I'll arrange for him to call on you in the morning."

"Oh no, I couldn't possibly put you to such trouble," Linnet exclaimed, though fading hope was rising once more. "But if you give me his direction—"

"It is no trouble," he insisted. "I pass his house on my way to retrieve my horse."

They were approaching the corner to High Street, leaving her little time to argue. Besides, she had no wish to appear ungrateful. "Then I thank you once more."

He tipped his hat to her and bowed. "There is no need. It's my pleasure. I hope I may call on your mother later this afternoon, if she is well enough."

Trying not to blush, Linnet said, "She will look forward to it. Goodbye, sir."

"Until later," he replied.

As she walked away from him, she couldn't help smiling into her veil. Somehow it didn't seem to matter that her business had been only half as successful as she expected.

Until she got home and discovered the letter from the boys' school, refusing to receive them for another term since the fees for last year had still not been paid.

>>>><<<<

FOR HER MOTHER'S sake, she changed into her best day gown—which was still somewhat old but at least the pale blue color suited her—and kept the smile pinned to her face. But all her pleasurable anticipation at seeing Mr. Wolfe again had got lost in anxiety.

The family's callers were rare, since they did not go out into society, and tended to be limited to elderly ladies encountered by her mother at the pump room. And indeed, one Miss Muir who had lived a large part of her life in Blackhaven, did call. She arrived at almost the same time as Fotheringham and a friend of his who affected a very odd style of necktie—some carelessly knotted red and white spotted thing.

While Miss Muir chatted with her mother and the children, both gentlemen put Linnet out of countenance by gazing at her with rapt attention. Bolton, lying by the fire under duress, returned the favor by staring back at both gentlemen with a constant growl in his throat. Linnet did not entirely blame him, but at least telling him off gave her somewhere else to look.

"I was telling Clifford here about our adventure yesterday," Sir Constantine announced. "I hope you are—"

"You must tell me also, when Bolton isn't listening," Linnet said nonsensically, her main purpose being to stop Sir Constantine talking on the subject. Rising, she changed her seat to one closer to the gentlemen, as though eager to hear their tale, which made both of them spring up and sit again like twin jack-in-the-boxes. Across the room, Laura giggled.

"Please don't mention yesterday's event in my mother's hearing," Linnet pleaded in a low voice. "I don't wish her to be upset."

Sir Constantine stared at her in astonishment. "You mean you have not told her? Depend upon it, the children will have!"

"Of course they have not," Linnet said indignantly. "And I really must ask for your discretion, sir. It did not previously occur to me, but I would rather this didn't get back to her through Blackhaven gossip either."

Sir Constantine looked devastated, and Linnet suspected he had already told several people the story with his own part in it somewhat embellished. She doubted Mr. Wolfe had figured very largely in his version.

"Of course, your wish must be my command," Sir Constantine said.

"And mine," Mr. Clifford said reverently. "Allow me to say, Miss Linnet, that you are as thoughtful and kind-hearted as you are fair."

Linnet regarded him with some doubt. As the eldest unmarried daughter, her correct mode of address was Miss James, not Miss Linnet. She could only suppose he had picked up the habit from Sir Constantine, who considered her Christian name most poetic.

"Are you also a poet, Mr. Clifford?" she asked.

"I scribble a little," Mr. Clifford said modestly, "but I cannot yet aspire to Fotheringham's standard."

Henry, overhearing this, caught Linnet's gaze and grinned openly. Linnet coughed and dragged her gaze back to Clifford's.

"I am honored," that young gentleman intoned, "that he has brought me to meet his muse. Allow me to say that I, too, now worship at your saintly feet, inspired, by your exquisite beauty, warmed by your glowing soul."

Linnet couldn't help her peel of laughter, just as the door opened and Hetty announced in disapproving tones, "Mr. Wolfe, ma'am."

Linnet's heart gave a funny little lurch. He strode in on Hetty's heels, and Linnet's smile widened as she jumped to her feet. Bolton leapt up at the same time, growling and lunging toward the latest visitor. Linnet had forgotten to order him to stay.

"Dear God," Sir Constantine said happily, apparently anticipating the inevitable blood with some pleasure.

"Linnet!" Laura squeaked in alarm.

"Sit!" Henry yelled.

Mr. Wolfe, however, merely held out his hand to the dog, who skidded to an untidy halt on the rug. "Good afternoon, Mr. Bolton," he said amiably.

The mastiff wagged his tail and licked Wolfe's fingers. As if unaware of the stunned silence in the room, Wolfe walked past him to Mrs. James and bowed.

"Mr. Wolfe," Linnet's mother managed, offering her frail hand. "It seems we are all delighted to see you, even Bolton!"

"Bolton and I have an understanding," Wolfe said, shaking hands, "not to eat each other without cause. How do you do, Mrs. James?"

While her mother introduced him to the others, Linnet made the best of her impulsive jump up to welcome him, by taking Bolton by the collar and walking him back to the hearth as though that was what she had intended all along.

"Where is Napoleon?" William asked eagerly. "Did you bring him with you?"

"Oh no, I have learned my lesson about Napoleon in polite society. I've left him in his cage and hope he won't escape."

"Napoleon has escaped?" Miss Muir gasped. "But I thought he was safely imprisoned on Elba!"

This set all the children into fits of laughter.

"Napoleon is Mr. Wolfe's pet monkey, ma'am," Linnet explained clearly to the deaf lady. "We came upon him the other day, and the children were most impressed."

"And you weren't?" Wolfe asked, turning his overwhelming gaze on her at last. Butterflies leapt in her stomach. "Poor Napoleon will be devastated."

"Good thing, too," Miss Muir said, and Wolfe's eyes lit with laughter.

"Shall I ring for tea, Mama?" Linnet asked breathlessly.

In the end, Hetty had to be sent for an extra cup and saucer, for Mrs. Grant the vicar's wife, also paid a surprise visit.

"Goodness, you have quite a houseful," she exclaimed, after greeting everyone. "I shan't intrude long, Mrs. James. It's just that I forgot completely when I saw you this morning…I have these." Taking her hand from her reticule, she produced several tickets with an air of triumph. "Vouchers for the assembly room ball," she explained to Linnet's baffled mother. "The manager is concerned by falling numbers since Christmas, and asked me to distribute these by way of temptation. I haven't seen you there before, so I hope I can entice by placing the vouchers in your hand."

Linnet's mother took them instinctively. "How good you are! But indeed, I don't believe I can manage such a long evening. I'm normally asleep by nine o'clock!"

"Well, if you feel like stretching it to ten, you could always drop in for an hour," Mrs. Grant coaxed.

"I would so like Linnet to go…"

Linnet smiled. "I don't care about such things."

"But you should," her mother insisted.

"I care far more that you don't exhaust yourself," Linnet retorted.

Mrs. Grant tapped her fingers on the arm of her

chair. "There is another alternative. If you feel able to part with Linnet for the evening, *I* could chaperone her."

"Oh no, we couldn't possibly put you out like that," Linnet said at once, though her mother looked thoughtful.

"We would love to have her company," Mrs. Grant coaxed. "But I would not deprive you of your main support if you need her!"

"Not at all, I have Laura and the boys," Linnet's mother said with decision. "I gratefully accept your kind offer."

"Excellent! Who else would like a voucher? Jack—I shan't stand on ceremony with you—here is one for you. Miss Muir? Gentlemen?"

Wolfe stood beside Linnet. "It appears we're going to the ball."

"I can't," Linnet said. "I have nothing to wear!"

"Of course you have," Laura argued. "When is it?"

"Friday," Mrs. Grant replied.

"Then you will definitely have something to wear," Laura said, by which Linnet finally understood that her sister, an excellent needlewoman at the tender age of thirteen, meant to work her magic on some existing garment.

Although not entirely convinced this would pass muster for such a fashionable event, Linnet did not have the heart to tell her so. Whatever Laura came up with for her, she would wear with pride.

"Won't you reserve the first waltz for me, Miss Linnet?" Sir Constantine pleaded.

"And the second for me?" Mr. Clifford begged.

Linnet laughed. "Goodness, I never remember such things. You must ask me at the time."

Shortly after, Miss Muir, who had stayed precisely half an hour, took her leave, followed somewhat reluctantly by the poets whose only hope of a worthwhile existence appeared to lie in Linnet's promise to go skating tomorrow morning.

"Skating where?" Wolfe asked when they had gone.

"Black Lake, close to your house, actually," Linnet replied, "although I don't *think* it's on your land! The lake is small—more of a pond—and froze over earlier this week."

"Ah yes, I saw people skating there when I rode into town this morning," Wolfe said.

"It was Lady Braithwaite's idea," Mrs. Grant said. "So we're having a select party!"

"But we can come, too?" William said anxiously.

"Oh, yes. Of course." Mrs. Grant rose to her feet. "And now I must go, before my monster awakes once more."

If she meant it as cue for Wolfe to leave, too, she was disappointed, for Wolfe, in conversation now with Henry while idly tickling Bolton's contented tummy, only remembered to rise to say goodbye as she passed him on her way to the door.

However, perhaps her departure reminded him of the impropriety of staying longer, for after only a few more minutes of idle banter with the children, he also took his leave. Remembering the question she wished to ask him in private, Linnet decided it was time to send Bolton into the back garden, and used it as excuse to walk downstairs with Wolfe.

"I don't suppose you have yet had the chance to speak to this other doctor?" she said as Bolton bounded ahead of them. "What was his name again?"

"Nicholas Lampton, and yes, I have left your mother's name with him."

"Thank you." She smiled fleetingly. "She enjoyed this afternoon, but she will be exhausted now, and sleep until dinner time."

"And what will you do?"

"Help her into bed and write some difficult letters. And then, I suppose, we shall take Bolton for a walk on the beach." Just for a moment, she thought she read an invitation in his eyes, but he only smiled at held out his hand.

"Then goodbye. And I may see you tomorrow, if the lake is still frozen and if I'm up before midday."

She placed her hand in his. "Will you bring Napoleon?"

"Do you think I should?"

"I think between them, he and Bolton could clear the ice."

"It might be worth it, then!"

CHAPTER SIX

D<small>R. LAMPTON ARRIVED</small> the following morning before her mother was even out of bed. Brisk and unexpectedly young, he sat down by the bed and asked a lot of questions, going back to when Mrs. James originally fell ill and the treatments and diets prescribed to her. Occasionally, a frown crossed his brow, but mostly, he listened without comment.

Only then did he examine her, first inspecting under her eyelids and then taking her pulse. He listened to her breathing.

"Can you help her, doctor?" Linnet asked.

"Yes, I believe so." He sat back in his chair and glanced from her to her mother. "But it will do no good if you are also following Dr. Bellamy's regime."

"My mother has already made up her mind not to consult Dr. Bellamy again," Linnet said.

Lampton did not reply that was a good thing, but Linnet had little doubt that was what he meant. "I can hear no sign of the original infection in your lungs. That seems to have cleared completely. You have been bled constantly for months, and it's my belief, your weakness stems from blood loss exacerbated by poor diet. That is what we must remedy."

"No more bleeding?" Linnet's mother said as if scarcely able to hope. "No leeches?"

"Absolutely *nothing* of that nature," Lampton assured her with a quick, rather charming smile. He bent and delved into his capacious bag, before holding up a bottle with an air of triumph. "Take a glass of this cordial night and morning. I'll send round some more later. Start now, if you please," he added to Linnet, who hastily poured some of the evil looking drink into a glass and handed it somewhat doubtfully to her mother.

"It tastes better than it looks," the doctor said without looking up from the paper on which he was busily writing. "These are the foods I want you to eat. No more gruels and less bland chicken soups. You need fresh red meat, lots of fresh vegetables, nuts, and fruits when you can get them. Small meals at a time is fine until your appetite returns, just make sure what you do eat is good. And you will still need plenty of rest. Only gentle exercise." He passed his list to Linnet and stood.

"And the waters?" Linnet asked.

He shrugged. "They'll do her no harm. Are you in Blackhaven for long?"

"Until the end of the month," Linnet replied.

"I'll call again in a week. But don't expect to be well again immediately. This will take time, but I believe you will be on the mend before you leave us. Good-bye!"

"Thank you, Doctor," Linnet said as she showed him out. She felt slightly bemused.

⇶⇶⇷⇷

WOLFE TOLD HIMSELF he was glad to escape the upheaval and racket of the house—for he had summoned people to repair the outside and clean up the inside. He extracted his old skates from the bottom of his trunk where he'd thrown them on the off-chance he'd need them since he was travelling in winter. Then, leaving Napoleon in his outside cage with a blanket and some nuts to crack, he saddled Nosey and rode out to the lake, which was indeed little more than a pond.

The James family were already there, easily picked out among the well-dressed throng who slid about the surface of the lake with varying degrees of skill. The children were very good, well-balanced and daring, although they had obviously been warned and avoided the center of the lake where the ice was likeliest to be thin. With them, were another two young girls of around Henry and Laura's ages.

It was only when his gaze finally landed on Linnet that he admitted to himself why he had really come. As he sat on the fallen tree trunk at the edge of the lake and began to strap his skates to his boots, he could not take his eyes off her. Graceful and laughing, she swept past her brothers, wobbled a bit over a bump in the ice and grabbed Henry. They both ended on their rears with untroubled good humor, helped each other to rise, and skated on in different directions.

He liked to look at her. He liked it too much, but more than that, she intrigued him wildly. She had so much to contend with—poverty, he suspected, a severe decline in her mother's health, and the care of her siblings, now and in the uncertain future. And yet, she faced it all with smiling courage and an interest in all life had to offer. No petulance, no tantrums or perverse determination to go the devil. He could learn a lot from her.

Rising, he stepped onto the ice. The last time he had skated had been last winter in the Pyrenees, on makeshift skates, racing with his fellow officers in a somewhat brutal rough and tumble that had left him bruised, victorious, and very happy. This was…different.

To begin with, Mrs. Grant and another young lady skated up to him escorted by a tall, handsome young man.

"Allow me to present Mr. John Wolfe, Lord Ottley's son, and an old friend of Tristram's. Jack, Lord and Lady Braithwaite, from the castle.

Wolfe bowed and shook hands with the earl.

"I'm acquainted with your father," Braithwaite said.

Wolfe murmured something polite, but in truth, the earl could not have said anything more guaranteed to set his back up. His restless gaze found Linnet again, skating now beside Constantine Fotheringham, who appeared to be very skilled.

As Wolfe excused himself, her laughter echoed across the lake and she swept away from Constantine toward the children once more. This brought her in Wolfe's direction. Seeing him, a spontaneous smile lit her face, and a wild new happiness seemed to rush up from his toes, filling him, so that he could not be still.

"Excuse me," he said, and pushed off to meet her and the children.

Still skating, he bowed on his approach and came to a halt in front of her. Up close, her skin was fresh and flushed with the cold, her lips red and luscious in their welcoming smile.

"Mr. Wolfe, Mr. Wolfe, can you do a figure of eight?" William demanded.

"Of course, he can," Henry said scornfully. "He's clearly the expert! Can you jump on the ice, sir?"

"I've never tried. But I can race you if you like—all of you! Back to the edge!"

Linnet joined in, too. But in the mad, laughing dash to the edge of the lake, William grew too determined to win and ended flat on his face on the snowy ground. Between them, Wolfe and Henry pulled him to his feet.

"I won!" he exclaimed with joy. "I won!"

"So you did," Wolfe agreed before Henry could dispute it. "By a length!"

"And now I wish to be more sedate," Linnet said, "for I have no breath left!"

As the children raced each other, he had a moment of gentle skating beside their sister.

"Thank you for Dr. Lampton," she said warmly. "My mother is quite taken with him, mostly because he does not wish to bleed her, but he is far more hopeful than Dr. Bellamy."

"I'm glad to hear it, but it is the Grants you have to thank, not me. I avoid doctors like the plague since one dug a ball out of my leg."

"I'm sure you should be more grateful."

"Oh, I am grateful. I just have no desire to remember let alone repeat, the experience."

"Then you must be glad to have left the army!"

He kept the smile in place. "Of course I must."

For an instant, her sharp eyes searched his, but she did not pry, merely remarked that it was growing crowded on the ice.

"Are all these people friends of Lady Braithwaite's?" he asked, examining the less well-dressed newcomers.

"I shouldn't think so. We seem to have a mix of two parties, now! Well, the lake is not on private land."

"It should be," Sir Constantine said with feeling, skating up in time to overhear her remark. "Why should you be forced to rub shoulders with the hoi polloi?"

Linnet laughed. "Oh, I am not forced. In most company, I probably *am* the hoi polloi!"

Sir Constantine refused to entertain such a ridiculous idea. As Clifford, the other young poet joined them, Wolfe quickly grew bored and skated off. Encountering Lord Braithwaite once more, he indulged in a race with him and an officer of the local regiment, around and through the throngs of new arrivals.

When he next looked around for Linnet, she was skating beside Clifford, who was over-solicitous in Wolfe's view, although Linnet didn't appear displeased by his company. Her siblings were mostly skating around Mrs. Grant and Lady Braithwaite, in company with the two girls he had seen with them before. William, however, was not with them.

A quick search discovered him in the midst of a new throng, skating with a boy of perhaps his own age. It was a little too crowded and a little too close to the middle of the lake, so Wolfe set off in his direction, meaning to guide him outward again.

However, Fotheringham seemed to be among this crowd, so no doubt Will would move to escape him. But William, deep in concentration of his feet, skating backward at high speed, did not even see Sir Constantine who was, in fact, being unusually discreet as he moved toward the boy.

If Wolfe had not been concentrating on the pair so hard, he would never have seen the incident. But some instinct he had learned not to ignore urged him closer with ever-greater speed. Even so, he could scarcely believe it when Fotheringham skated right into the boy, actively pushing him toward the center of the lake before skating on into the crowd.

William went down on the ice with a thud which dragged more attention to him. Wolfe, pushing his way through, heard the faint crackling of the ice, saw the split appear as William jumped to his feet. He seemed to rock and then slid straight downward as the ice broke.

With a growl, Wolfe shoved two gawping young men aside and dropped flat on his belly. "Get back to the edges!" he shouted to those nearest and scooted forward to the floundering Henry. Fotheringham swooped across the ice to the crack, calling, "I'm coming, I'm coming!" The moron was cracking the ice further, an outcome he noted with a sudden cry as he swerved away again.

Henry, up to his waist in the freezing water, clung onto the edge of the ice. The startlement in his eyes was just turning to terrified understanding, when Wolfe reached out to him.

"I've got you," he soothed, catching him under both armpits. "I've got you."

Henry let out a sob as Wolfe lifted him out of the water and dragged him on his back for several feet before rising with him in his arms and skating furiously for the edge of the lake.

The ice was clearing rapidly. Only Linnet skated toward him, her face white with fear.

"He's fine," Wolfe assured her. "But he needs warmth and dry clothes."

"Yours is the nearest house," Mrs. Grant said.

"Put him in the cart," Linnet commanded.

"Only to get those freezing clothes off him. Wrap him in as many dry blankets as you can find and I'll ride with him to the house. You can follow."

She didn't argue, merely reached for her shaking brother's scarf and coat before Wolfe had even laid him in the cart and whistled for Nosey while he kicked off his skates.

>>><<<

LINNET HAD NEVER been more frustrated with the slow pace of the pony, even with Mrs. Grant riding in front. Linnet drove the old cart with Laura and Henry beside her, remaining calm for their sakes, and yet unable to help her mind rolling through terrible possibilities.

As though sensing an end to his labors, the pony picked up speed as they approached the house. Men swarmed off the roof to take care of the pony, which surprised Linnet in the small part of her mind not wrapped up in her brother's accident.

An unknown woman in a mob cap opened the front door before they even reached it. "You must be Miss James, come right in, ma'am...the door down the passage on the right there. Oh good afternoon to you, Mrs. Grant."

Linnet flew down the passage to the room where they had first encountered Mr. Wolfe and threw open the door, all but knocking over their host who had clearly been on his way to meet them. "Is he...?"

Her eyes flew to a movement on the sofa which had been pulled close to the roaring fire in the hearth. Henry sat there, propped up on cushions and wrapped cozily in blankets. Hanging around his neck and peeping out from under the blanket, was Napoleon the Barbary monkey.

Henry grinned hugely. "Look, Linny, he likes me! He's so cuddly and warm as toast!"

Linnet let out a laugh that was part sob and rushed over to him. "Oh, thank God! Are you feeling warm again?" Clutched in both his hands was a rough, steaming mug of what looked like hot chocolate.

"Right as rain," Henry said cheerfully, grinning over Linnet's shoulder at his other siblings. He brought his gaze back to her as she sniffed. "You didn't need to come—" He broke off, eyeing her suspiciously. "Linnet, you're not *crying*, are you?"

Linnet swiped her eyes on her glove. "Of course, I'm not, ridiculous boy. It's just the thought of all that freezing cold water brings the tears to my eyes." She held out two fingers to the monkey. "Thank you, Napoleon, for looking after my little brother."

Napoleon's furry hand stretched out and grasped hers, then slid back around Henry's neck. He drew back his lips in a grin. Linnet cleared out of the way to let her siblings also shake Napoleon's hand, and turned to meet Wolfe's gaze.

"I don't know how to thank you."

"There is nothing to thank me for," he said at once. "But we do need to talk."

"About Henry?" she demanded at once.

"No, no, I'm sure Henry will be fine, though you might ask Dr. Lampton to check on him just to be sure." He hesitated, glancing toward Mrs. Grant who stood by the closed door.

"I'll sit with the children," Mrs. Grant said at once, moving into the room, "but if the monkey runs loose, I may scream."

"I've rarely seen him look so comfortable," Wolfe murmured as he opened the door and ushered Linnet out before him. "Lord, nowhere is quiet! I know, in here to the front room. Molly has already cleaned it, so we should have an hour before she rehangs the curtains."

Wolfe ushered her into the large room through whose grubby windows she had once tried to peer. Now they were bright and sparkling outside and in, and she realized it was a pleasant, well-proportioned apartment, the walls half-paneled in wood, and rather fine decorative cornicing.

"What a beautiful room," she exclaimed.

"It has scrubbed up quite well," he agreed, subjecting it to a critical appraisal. "I thought it would be very dark with all that wood, but the light is just right." Leaving the door open, he followed her into the room and invited her to sit. "Tell me about Fotheringham."

From the sofa, she regarded his looming figure in some surprise. "I doubt I can add anything you have not already observed for yourself."

He dragged his hand through his hair and tugged once. "Do you have any intention of marrying him?"

She flushed, half-annoyed at the personal nature of the question, and yet half-hopeful that it was inspired by jealousy. *Jealousy? What is the matter with me?* "None. But then, to be fair, he has not asked me."

"He is very desperate for your attention. And he is a wealthy man who could solve many of your family's problems."

She sprang to her feet before she knew what she was doing. "How dare you? How *dare* you!"

He took a step nearer and took her hand. In fury, she tried to tug it free but he held on. "There, be still. It is not my intention to insult or upset you."

"I am not upset," she raged with patent untruth, "but intended or otherwise, the insult was most definitely there!"

An impatient frown tugged down his dark brow. "Then I apologize. I merely wondered how softly I needed to phrase this."

"Phrase what?"

"Come, sit," he said, handing her to the sofa once more. After a moment's hesitation, she sat on the very edge, her back stiff and straight to show her disapproval. He sat beside her, half-turned to face her. "William doesn't really know what happened on the ice—he just felt someone slam into him, and he was thrown onto the thin ice at the center. But *I* know. I saw everything. Fotheringham did it quite deliberately."

"*Fotheringham?* Don't be ridiculous! Why would he do such a thing? *Particularly* if he wishes to curry favor with me."

"Because he meant to save William. I doubt he expected the ice to break. The point is, he put your brother at risk just for the chance of your finally taking him seriously."

"You must be mistaken," Linnet said impatiently.

"There is also the matter of the hold-up," Wolfe added.

Fresh unease began to seep into her heart. Sir Constantine had been there, too.

Wolfe said, "He hired the supposed footpads to hold you up and flee when he rode to the rescue."

"You can't possibly know that—"

"I found one of them in the tavern. I do know it. I didn't mean to say anything to you about it, but today's 'accident' changes all that. Linnet, the man's obsession is dangerous. You must beware of him."

"Thank you, I am wary of everyone." Which is when it popped into her head that Wolfe, too, had been present at both events, and that the rescuing had been done not by Fotheringham but by *him*. Thus, inclining her in Wolfe's favor. She shook her head impatiently. "But this is silly. I am no one. My family is neither great nor wealthy. We have no influence."

"I don't believe he cares for such things."

"Do you?" she asked.

He met her gaze, and she saw at once that he knew exactly what she meant. Shame and embarrassment seeped through her veins.

He rose to his feet. "No, as it happens. But my father does."

"Have I offended you?" she asked bluntly. "I'm afraid I'm in the habit of thinking aloud. To be frank, your behaving in such a way for such a reason seems even more ridiculous than Sir Constantine doing so."

He bowed ironically. "Don't discount Fotheringham. You are his muse, and he is not exactly balanced. Whatever my motives, do you believe that I will look out for your family?"

"You already have." She rubbed her forehead as if that could clear her mind. "You must think me appallingly ungrateful to say what I did."

He shrugged. "You don't know me. And I am not a good man."

"You have been good to *us*," she said, rising and offering her hand. "And I thank you with all my heart."

His gaze dropped to her hand, and for a moment, she thought he would not take it, that he would merely bow coldly and walk away. But after an instant, his fingers curled around hers, and he bent, pressing his lips briefly to her hand. A pleasurable little shock ran up her arm and ended somewhere in the pit of her stomach.

"Don't," he said ruefully and dropped her hand. "We had best return to the others."

Teased by the other children, Napoleon was half out of William's blanket.

Wolfe strode up and covered him again. "You're losing your warming pan."

William laughed. "He's very hairy and wriggly for a warming pan!"

Linnet glanced from him to the window. Snow had begun to fall, not in great flurries, but enough to remind her how cold it was already, and how cold it would get when daylight faded.

Mrs. Grant said, "You're wondering whether to dare take him out again in the cold today."

"I own I would rather not, but I see no alternative."

"He can stay here, if you wish," Wolfe said.

"Oh, may I, Linnet?" William asked eagerly. "Please!"

"I don't see how. For even if I was to defy convention and stay with you, there is Mama to consider.

"Hetty can manage Mama," Henry suggested. "You've already bought her dinner and she will easily remember the cordial."

"That isn't the *whole* point," Linnet said.

"How is this?" Wolfe interrupted. "Mrs. Grant will drive Henry and Laura back to Blackhaven with a letter from you. They will then be able to keep your mother company and do whatever is necessary for her. I will remove for the night to the White Lion, and Molly will stay here to look after you and William."

"Oh no," Linnet demurred. "We could not possibly put you out like that."

"Will Napoleon stay here?" William asked at the same time.

"Will!" Linnet scolded.

Wolfe's lips twitched. "Of course he will. One of us will have to stay to carry out the duties of host."

William grinned.

"I suppose you did get a terrible soaking," Laura said grudgingly, "So I suppose it's only fair you get the fun as well."

Despite her instinctive protest, Linnet could see that it was the best possible solution.

CHAPTER SEVEN

"**I** SHALL SEND my closed carriage for you both tomorrow morning," Mrs. Grant offered only half an hour later as she swept Laura and Henry to the front door. "And I'll see if Dr. Lampton can come out to look at William this afternoon."

"He will be sick of the sight of us," Linnet said ruefully. "Two free consultations in one day."

"Free?" Mrs. Grant repeated in clear surprise.

"Mr. Wolfe said…" She broke off as understanding dawned. Her mother's consultation was *not* free. Wolfe meant to settle the bill. Outrage battled with gratitude and won, while she forced a smile to her lips. "Never mind. I will have had the wrong end of the stick, as usual. Thank you so much for this, Mrs. Grant. Henry, do you have my letter to Mama? Laura, you must help Hetty all you can and make sure Mama takes the cordial tonight and before breakfast tomorrow morning…"

As Linnet waved them off in the cart, Mrs. Grant's mare, ambling along beside it at the end of a leading rein, she became aware of Wolfe's presence beside her.

"You lied to me," she said.

He didn't pretend to misunderstand. Probably he had overheard her brief conversation with Kate Grant. "I, too, conducted business at the pawnshop. In a moment of weakness, I decided your mother was more important than another night's gambling and drinking. If you really want to, you can pay me back when things are better."

"But you have debts, too, do you not?" she argued.

"I'm juggling what I have."

"It isn't right," she said intensely. And yet the alternative, letting her mother die, was not a possibility she could contemplate.

"In the eyes of the world. For myself, I see no problem in friends helping each other out when they can."

She met his gaze. "But we aren't friends. We barely know each other. And from my point of view, the helping has been very one-sided."

"No." He did not elaborate, merely urged her back into the warmth of the house.

They discovered Molly laying down the law to the

two village girls who were helping her clean. "If you want to leave here before dark, then you'd better work twice as fast, because you're not going anywhere until those two bedrooms are clean and warm!"

"Molly, one bedroom would do for William and me," Linnet called. "If a trundle bed or sofa was available, that would be wonderful. I would rather be there with him to notice any change."

"There you are," Molly said severely to the girls. "Now, get on with it. Sorry, Miss, the stupid creatures are convinced the house is haunted.

"Aren't you?" Wolfe asked.

Molly laughed. "Lord, no, who's to haunt it? There's been no one living or dying here for a hundred years!"

"I'm not sure I believe that," Linnet said as they went back to William. "Neither the furnishings nor the paint are a hundred years old!"

"I suspect it was checked up on and rented periodically, but it has been pretty much ignored by my family. I only discovered I owned it a couple of months ago."

Rejoining William, they found Napoleon had grown quite agitated in their absence. Apparently, he was desperate to go to his cage where, Wolfe told her without embarrassment, he preferred to perform his bodily functions, even when he was wearing a napkin as now.

While Wolfe took him away, Linnet sat on a chair close to William's sofa.

"How are you feeling?" she asked, searching his face for signs of fever or distress.

"Warm and a little fuzzy," William replied. "In a good way, so don't fuss!"

"I never fuss," Linnet said with dignity.

William grinned. "I know you don't. You are the best of sisters. I'm feeling stupid, if you want the truth, trying to think how I came to fall through the ice."

"Mr. Wolfe said someone bumped into you."

"By Jove, yes, hard, too." He frowned. "But I was skating *away* from the center. It almost felt like some *force* dragged me there."

"The force of the bump must have pushed you very hard. Did you see who knocked into you?"

His frown deepened but he shook his head. "No, he came from the side, though, where the biggest crowd of people was. I don't understand how I slid in the direction I did. Everyone was gawping or rushing the other way. I knew the ice had broken and I was going in. And then I saw Mr. Wolfe skating toward me at break-neck speed. And your knight of then pen! He was nearer, and I remember thinking it was pretty brave of him to try and help when everyone else was either gawking or rushing away. And I thought Mr. Wolfe fell, but he didn't, did he? He lay on the ice to spread his weight so it wouldn't crack further." He shivered. "It was so cold, though, it *hurt*."

She leaned forward and ruffled his hair. "I know. You were very brave."

Wolfe came back in, and they played a rather hilarious game of "Twenty Questions"–where one person pretended to be someone or something and the others had to guess who or what by asking questions. Over the game, the slightly tense atmosphere between Linnet and their host seemed to relax into friendly fun. By the time Dr. Lampton arrived, it was almost as if she had known him forever, that he was one of the family.

The doctor asked William what had happened, but did not scold. Linnet suspected he already knew from Kate. He pronounced Will well enough but gave her a potion to help reduce any fever that might develop overnight.

"And unless his condition changes," he told Linnet, "he will be fine to travel back to Blackhaven tomorrow."

Linnet stayed with William while Wolfe showed the doctor out. She only realized her error seconds before Wolfe returned.

"I hope you did not tell him to send you *this* bill, too," she said, scowling at him.

His eyes teased her somewhat lazily. "I didn't mention anything so vulgar."

And she could not help laughing. "Of course, you did not. Forgive me!"

Shortly afterward, Molly brought in a very decent dinner. Wolfe moved the table closer to the fire, and Linnet was delighted to see Will eat with his usual gusto.

Once Molly had cleared the plates away, they played cards and chatted until William fell asleep.

"He's had a rather more exciting day than he bargained for," Linnet said.

"I think we all have."

She smiled. "After the life you have led on the Peninsula and in France, I imagine rescuing a child from the ice and playing Twenty Questions with him doesn't rate very highly as excitement."

The candlelight played across his lean face, lending it both warmth and mystery. She took comfort in his company, and yet it held a danger she couldn't quite understand.

He said, "I'm beginning to think there are many forms of excitement. Many kinds of battle."

"What do you mean?" she asked.

Although his gaze did not leave her, there was a distance in his eyes as though his thoughts were far from this room. "War is in my blood. The founder of our family, the great knight William de Wolfe, won land and wealth through his fighting prowess, a fortune that we still hold today in various family branches. But very few of us over the centuries ever settled down to be landlords or government ministers. We're still restless and violent under the veneer of modern civilization. I always knew that, learned early on how to channel my own into sport and then the army."

He smiled reminiscently. "From the beginning, I loved everything about war. Strategy, tactics, the joy of battle, and the challenge of coming out of it with as many men as possible. I even loved the spells of boredom because I used them to plan to do better. Civilian life was distant, dull, and I could never imagine going back to it."

"Then why did you?" she asked curiously.

He shrugged. "A promise I made my father when he bought me my first commission. To get it, I had to swear I would sell out as soon as the war was over. I'm his heir, you see. He never envisaged the war lasting so long, of course, but when Bonaparte abdicated, he wrote to me, reminding me of my promise, my duty, my responsibilities."

His eyes cleared and refocused on her with a fleeting smile. "I kept to the letter of my promise. I sold out and came home. But the duties, the responsibilities he wants me to undertake seem so trivial compared with those I've known. I need to be fighting or at least planning to fight, and so, I've been going to the devil because I don't like my new life. Because, like a petulant child, I resent it being inflicted upon me."

"Perhaps you need to go back to the army."

"There's no enemy to fight."

"Not right now, but I'm sure there will be soon enough!"

"Perhaps. But as I say, there are many kinds of

battle. For example, think what a fight it would be to whip not only this house, but this land into shape, to make it support tenants and pay me."

For some reason this pleased her and she couldn't help smiling. "Then you are considering *not* selling?"

"Considering. But the estate is not large. My father has other properties. Perhaps learning to manage them is a good fight, too."

"With your people almost like the soldiers who depended on you before."

"The dependence is just as real. The outcome, good or ill, is still vital."

She nodded thoughtfully. "It is a good way to look at things. What changed your view?"

He smiled. "You did."

Astonishment widened her eyes, but her question died in her throat. Suddenly, he took her breath away, just by looking at her. She felt as if some bond were winding around her, drawing her close to him, and there was nowhere she wanted to be more.

He rose slowly to his feet, and her heart thundered as he came closer. She could not move.

He bent. "I'll carry him up to bed before I go."

As he lifted William in his arms, blankets and all,

her breath rushed out. She almost laughed at herself.

"Thank you," she managed. "I doubt he'll wake very easily."

She followed him out of the room and upstairs to the bedchamber Molly and her minions had prepared. She turned up the lamp, then went to turn back the covers on the bed so that Wolfe could lay her brother beneath them. She moved the warming pan which had made the sheets cozy and pleasant to the touch. Will grunted but didn't wake.

Linnet followed him back downstairs to the front door. "I'm sorry to eject you from your own house in this weather. Surely no one would know or care if you stayed."

He turned, too close to her. His eyes burned in a way that churned her inside out. She suspected she had said something wrong and easily misunderstood, but at that moment, she could not think what.

"*I* would know," he said huskily. "God knows, I would." He bent his head. His hand cupped her cheek and he kissed her lips, very softly, very gently, and yet heat surged through her, depriving her of breath.

She stared up at him as he raised his head, aware she should be outraged. But as his hand slid away from her face, she reached up in panic and caught it, pressing it to her cheek once more. From sheer instinct, sheer desire, she lifted her face to his once more.

An inarticulate sound escaped him, and then he swopped, seizing her mouth in a very different kiss, fierce and yet tender, invasive and yet exciting, sweet and completely overwhelming. She could only cling to his coat and his lips and pray for it never to stop.

But it did. "And that," he said shakily, "is the real reason I cannot stay."

His mouth pressed hers once more, and then he released her to seize his bag from the floor and his great coat from the stand. The door opened and closed behind him before she even realized what had just happened.

In wonder, she touched her lips, felt them smile tremulously under her fingertips. She should be ashamed, but she wasn't. Her heart soared.

⫯⫯⫯⫰⫰⫰

IN THE MORNING, Molly brought them both hot chocolate to drink in bed. William, apparently none the worse for his adventure, couldn't wait to get dressed and see Napoleon again.

They were still eating breakfast when Mrs. Grant arrived and pronounced herself delighted to see William so well. As they finished hastily, thanked Molly profusely, and bundled William into the coach, very well-wrapped up, Linnet couldn't help feeling piqued that Wolfe had not returned to wave them off.

He had kissed her…and in such a way, admitting temptation. He liked her, she knew he did. He had stayed talking to her long after civility demanded he remain, even after Will had fallen asleep. He had told her things from his heart.

But perhaps he regretted the kisses, either because he did not really mean them—gentlemen often didn't, according to her mother—or because it wasn't a terribly honorable thing to have done. After all, her family might have been poor, but she *was* a lady.

Still, she was not worthy to marry a wealthy baron's heir.

Marry? She gave herself a mental slap. Where had that thought even come from? They barely knew each other. And yet what she did know, she liked. She had never met anyone like Jack Wolfe and suddenly the idea that she would never see him again appalled and

terrified her. Some profound, sweet feeling overwhelmed her, and she quite lost track of Mrs. Grant
and William's conversation.

Was she falling in love with Jack Wolfe?

Happiness burst inside her. *I do love him. I love
him already. And he kissed me.*

For a moment, she became lost in the memory of
his kisses. And then harsh reality broke through her
happiness like a knife. He would not, could not marry
her, so what did he mean by kissing her?

No wonder he was keeping out of her way.

CHAPTER EIGHT

A LTHOUGH CLOSELY WATCHED by his whole household for the smallest signs of a chill, fever, cough, or other infection, William remained perfectly healthy. On the afternoon they returned to Blackhaven, several people called to ask after his health until he quite preened under all the attention.

Sir Constantine and Mr. Clifford were among their callers that day. Linnet, remembering Wolfe's accusations against him, watched him carefully. He did seem genuinely concerned for Will, and she could only think that Wolfe was mistaken, especially when William thanked him for trying to save him and he blushed. Or was that shame for having caused the accident in the first place?

"Are you looking at him in a new light?" Laura murmured in her ear.

"I don't quite know," Linnet replied.

"You are aware that if you could only bring yourself to marry him, all our troubles would be at an end?"

Linnet jerked her head around to stare at her little sister. "I beg your pardon?"

"Well they would," Laura said defiantly. "We'd live in a beautiful house—probably several beautiful houses!—the boys could go to a decent school and I could be presented at court and have a London season."

Linnet made an effort and closed her mouth, swallowing back her instinctive retort. "Where on earth did you get such ideas?"

"I heard Mrs. Grant's coachman telling Hetty," Laura confessed. "He said we could be rich if we wanted to, that you were quite at fault for being so selfish as not to encourage him."

"And what did Hetty reply?" Linnet asked wrathfully.

"She boxed his ears," Laura admitted.

"And from this, you believe you are in the right to repeat such things?"

Laura flushed. "Oh well, it was just a thought. You needn't chew my head off."

"Well, I won't while we have guests, but if you dare repeat—"

"Oh, I won't. Be easy!"

In truth, she was very far from easy. Until they had come to Blackhaven and met Sir Constantine, it had never entered her head that she could save the family through marriage. And although she could not take him seriously as a prospective husband, the idea did occur that if she could only meet another rich—or even just *comfortable* man—who liked her, she might fall in love with him and carry her family with her into good fortune.

Unfortunately, since they rarely went into society, she never met any likely candidates, and the vague thought at the back of her head had remained just that. She had never once considered that in rejecting Sir Constantine she was being selfish. Surely to marry a man for such reasons was vulgar, unkind, and demeaning to them both?

Jack Wolfe's face swam through her mind and was quickly banished. She must not think of him. She must not… Oh, why didn't he come?

But he did not call that day, and the next, by the time they had eaten luncheon, she gave up. It was the assembly room ball tonight, so she doubted there would be many calls.

Laura had very cleverly altered one of her mother's old gowns, an amber silk, into a more fashionable ball gown, cutting the worn hem right away to reveal a white underdress embellished with pleats and tiny sparkling crystals.

"You'll look golden and beautiful," Laura said, smiling.

"It's delightful," Linnet assured her, genuinely awed. "You are the cleverest creature!"

"I am pleased with it! And your pearls will be just right."

Linnet smiled vaguely, for the family did not yet know she had pawned them. "Of course."

She was glad of Hetty's interruption. "A word, if you please, Miss Linnet."

Linnet hastily left the bedchamber she shared with her sister, following Hetty to the top of the stairs, where the maid turned to face her with pursed lips.

"That gentleman is here asking for you. Shall I send him about his business?"

"What gentleman?" Linnet asked, bewildered. "Isn't he with Mama?"

"No, he won't go up, says he's in a hurry but has to see you."

"Oh dear, if Sir Constantine—"

"Not him," Hetty interrupted. "Mr. Wolfe!"

Linnet's heart turned over with a thud. "Thank you." She hurried downstairs, trying to keep her breath even.

She saw him at once, just inside the front door, impatiently tapping one glove against his boot. He stilled when he caught sight of her.

She walked along the hall to him as calmly as she could. "Mr. Wolfe, won't you come up to my mother?"

"Ah, no, I told your maid I can't stop, but I'm glad to have caught you. She said you had probably gone out."

"No, but—" She turned, following the direction of Wolfe's gaze to Hetty, who stood glaring at him from the foot of the stairs. "That will be all, Hetty," she said firmly.

The maid sniffed and walked reluctantly toward the kitchen.

"How is William?" he asked.

"Ripe for trouble and apparently none the worse," she replied. "He will be sorry to miss you."

He nodded once, as though that couldn't be helped, and drew his hand from his pocket. "I have something for you, but I don't want to give you it in public."

"What is it?" she asked, regarding the brown paper parcel he held out to her.

"It's yours."

Puzzled, she took the little parcel, and his other hand closed over hers. "There are a few things I need to do, but we'll talk tonight."

She couldn't help smiling. "You *will* go to the ball?"

"I will." His hand tightened. "I have something particular to ask you. All I need is hope." He bent, raising their joined hands, and crushed his lips to her wrist. "Until tonight."

And then he was gone, the door slamming shut behind him.

Linnet stared after him, unseeing. Her hand crept to her galloping heart. *I have something particular to ask you.* Was it possible? Gasping, she turned and ran back upstairs before anyone could see her with the parcel. She entered the bedchamber with it grasped behind her back, but Laura had gone, leaving the ball gown spread over the back of a chair.

Linnet threw herself on her bed and untied the parcel, Inside was a leather case she had never seen before. Opening it, she discovered a necklace she knew only too well. Her grandmother's pearls.

Somehow, he had bought them back for her.

She had never trusted that pawnbroker.

She touched the pearls, swallowing the tears in her throat. "Thank you," she whispered. Even though it was not right, she was grateful, as she was in truth, for everything else he had done for her and her family. It could only mean he cared for her. And tonight, he was going to ask her…

The growing smile froze on her lips. Ask her what?

Barons' heirs did not ask penniless ladies with no connections to marry them. Was he not…*buying* her? As even Cornelius Fotheringham had never attempted. She was *so* indebted to him now.

Not that she truly believed he would use such a debt to compel her. He was merely making her comfortable before he offered…not marriage but a carte blanche.

⫸⫷

WOLFE HAD RUSHED off from Linnet with the express purpose of catching up with Sir Constantine Fotheringham. He had glimpsed him in the coffee house window on his way to the James's house, and he already knew the man could be hard to find. He had tried most of yesterday.

Fortunately, Fotheringham and Clifford were just emerging from the coffee house, each clutching notes, no doubt of their latest poetical works.

"Gentlemen," Wolfe said with a slight bow.

Interrupted, both gentlemen looked up with irritation. Fotheringham's expression changed quickly to alarm.

"Wolfe," he said nervously, returning the bow but already moving on.

"You are a difficult man to pin down," Wolfe observed. "Did you not receive the message I left at the hotel?"

"Did I?" Fotheringham said vaguely. "My mind is so much on other things, on my muse, you know, that I forget—"

"Well, it is your muse I have come to speak to you about," Wolfe said cheerfully. "Come, let us walk to the beach, which I'm sure is a great source of inspiration. Good day, Clifford."

Fotheringham cast a pleading glance over his shoulder at his friend as Wolfe ruthlessly bore him off. But Clifford clearly felt unable to interfere. Wolfe could hear his swift footsteps walking away. Pleased, Wolfe turned his full attention to Fotheringham. He hadn't decided exactly the best method to proceed. That depended on the man himself. Certainly, he was looking anxious and uncertain.

"You think me a man of violence," Wolfe observed. "And I suppose I am. I was a soldier for eight years and I'm not afraid of a fight."

"I am a man of peace," Fotheringham assured him.

"Are you?" Wolfe caught and held his wide gaze. "I doubt many people would judge paying someone to hold up a carriage full of children at gunpoint as peaceful. Nor shoving a small boy onto thin ice and risking his life."

There was definitely fear in the poet's eyes now, but behind that lay more bewilderment than defiance. As though he knew his actions would be disapproved of but didn't quite understand why.

"Most people," Wolfe observed, "would consider that more violent and certainly more reprehensible than punching a rival in the nose."

"You don't understand," Fotheringham said, with a rather desperate attempt at loftiness. "She is my muse, my love. I would do anything to win her."

"Well, you won't do it by frightening her family or drowning her brother," Wolfe said brutally. He took Fotheringham's arm, urging him down the steps to the sandy beach that ran along the front of the town from the harbor. Fotheringham didn't resist. "In point of fact," Wolfe said, "you won't win her at all."

Fotheringham clutched his heart. "Not win her? I would rather end my life!"

"Nonsense," said Wolfe. "You are, first and foremost, a poet, a man who sees things just a little differently from the rest of us mere mortals. I understand that. But what does a man like that, a man like *you*, want with such mundane things as a wife and a parcel of noisy children? Nothing more guaranteed to disturb peaceful walks and moments of sublime inspiration than children playing pirates over your knees or your wife demanding you pay attention to the trivia of her day and the household bills you have not remembered to settle."

Fotheringham looked stunned, and then thoughtful.

"You don't want a lover or a wife, do you?" Wolfe said. "You want a lady on a pedestal to worship and inspire your love poetry. This is fortunate, for the lady in question will be *my* lover, *my* wife, and if anything further were to happen to her or to any members of her family—including Bolton—it would be my duty to take immediate action."

Fotheringham rubbed at his heart again. "Tell me it isn't so," he said in what seemed genuine distress.

"Oh, it *is* so," Wolfe said. "But don't be downhearted my friend. Or at least, don't give up the poetry. The lady may still sit on her pedestal and figure in your poetry—providing you neither name her nor touch her." He smiled faintly. "I have heard it said that there is nothing more helpful to a poet than being in love—except a broken heart."

That went home as he'd known it would. Fotheringham's expression was wide-eyed and hopeful. And yet incredible sadness was forming in his eyes.

There was nothing stranger than character. It was fortunate he had learned so much about men and their often-bizarre motivations. He did not think Fotheringham was a bad man, but he was obsessive and single-minded and almost entirely without empathy.

"You cannot trick or force people to feel the way you want them to," Wolfe said. "I should avoid anything else in that line should you find another muse, for I shall hear of it and I won't be able to let it go. As for the lady we were speaking of, she is under my protection from this moment. Do you understand?"

"I understand. I will never love again."

"It's the pain that makes you strong," Wolfe said gravely and held out his hand.

Fotheringham nodded and looked at the hand for a long moment before he took it. "Does she love you?"

"Yes, she loves me." He spoke with the certainty of her kisses in his heart. And yet, as he walked away from Fotheringham, uncertainty began to eat at him. They had known each other only a few days. And he had kissed many women without actually loving them. He was fairly sure most of them had kissed him in a similar spirit. So why was he so sure of Linnet?

He had no right to be. Because no woman had ever affected him like this before, his own certainty, his own mad rush of feeling had made him foolishly over-confident of Linnet's.

AS HER MOTHER, Laura, and Hetty all helped her prepare for the ball, Linnet was in an agony of conflicting feelings and indecision. A gently bred, well-brought-up girl, she was aware of her worth and the difference between right and wrong. On the other hand, she was also a realist. And if people—any people—expected her to marry Constantine Fotheringham without love, just for his money, why should she not accept the lesser proposal of a carte blanche from a man she *did* love?

It would not be so very different. She would have those kisses she yearned for, and even more intimate loving with the man who made her heart sing with a smile. She would be mistress of her own house, her family would, no doubt, be financially secure...although no longer received by anyone with any pretensions to polite society. And therein lay the rub. The family could either have poverty and respectability or notoriety and a physician's care for her mother. Surely such a position would ruin Laura's chances of a decent match.

She didn't know if it was pride or common sense arguing against accepting Wolfe's offer. She did know that part of her, a wicked, adventurous, sensual part, was very tempted. If she refused him, could she really bear him to walk away? And if he did so, surely, he was unworthy of her love, which was the most terrible thing of all.

I don't know him.

"Where are the pearls?" Laura demanded.

Linnet had known she would and she didn't want to answer. It seemed wrong to wear them. To do so would appear to endorse Wolfe's redeeming them for her. and might even seem to signal her acceptance of the carte blanche he was about to offer her. Besides, if they had remained at the pawnbroker's, she certainly couldn't have worn them.

She said casually, "I don't think I need them with this gown."

"Oh yes," her mother disputed. "They are exactly right for this dress."

Linnet hesitated a moment longer, but in truth, this was not a battle that needed to be fought now. She opened the drawer and took the pearls out of their old case. The other, she had hidden among her under-clothes. Her mother clasped the necklace about her throat and, smiling, turned her toward the glass.

A stranger with elegant hair, a swan-like neck and hectic, sparkling eyes stared back at her.

"You look beautiful," Laura said, awed.

"But worried," her mother added.

Linnet managed to laugh. "If I'm beautiful tonight, it's because of you, Laura, and your clever needle! And I can't help being a little worried, for I haven't been to many balls and I shall hate to be ignored when everyone else is dancing."

"Sir Constantine will dance with you," Laura said pertly.

"And Mr. Wolfe, surely," said their mother.

"But Mr. Wolfe is poor," Laura pointed out.

"He won't be forever," their mother said. "He is his father's heir. In any case, since when did you become so vulgar that you judge people by their wealth?"

"Since we didn't have any," Laura said tartly. Then she laughed and hugged her mother. "I'm only teasing both of you. I don't mean it. I hope they both dance with you, Linny and lots of other men, too. I won't sleep until you come home and tell me all about it!"

"Well, be sure to look after Mama," Linnet instructed. "Help her into bed and remember her cordial! Then do as Hetty bids you."

"Yes, yes," Laura said impatiently, going to the window. "Oh, here is Mrs. Grant's carriage. It hardly seems worth it to go along the road and round the corner!"

"It is in this weather," Mrs. James pointed out. "Off you go, my dear!"

Duly admired by her brothers who waited, grinning on the stairs, Linnet descended, and Hetty placed her mother's old evening cloak about her shoulders before opening the front door.

Mrs. Grant, who was surprisingly lavish for a vicar's wife, had her servant conduct Linnet from the front door to the waiting carriage under an umbrella to keep the falling snow off her. Mr. Grant was introduced to her but there was scarcely any time to get to know him before the short drive was completed. A line of carriages waited to disgorge passengers at the assembly room doors, but this, too, moved quickly, and once again the servant with the umbrella appeared to conduct the ladies inside.

"I know, I know, ridiculous to keep a servant for such a purpose," Mrs. Grant murmured. "But he has other duties, too, you know."

"I find him a lot more helpful than ridiculous!" Linnet said.

They entered into a large, gracious foyer. Mrs. Grant immediately led her toward a cloakroom where they would change their shoes, while Mr. Grant, hailing an old friend who was not Mr. Wolfe, waited for them.

Of course, the Grants knew everyone in Blackhaven and its surroundings, so it was not surprising that all eyes turned in their direction as they were announced. Several people greeted them as they walked into the bright, sparkling ballroom and took their seats.

Lord and Lady Braithwaite, whom she had met ice skating, sat at the next table to theirs, along with the earl's lovely young sister Lady Maria. Lady Braithwaite leaned over and asked after Henry. In moments, the two tables had become one, and Linnet was making friends with Maria, who was a little younger than her but very far from silly. In fact, she had a rather attractive, almost tragic sensitivity in her eyes that made Linnet want to look after her. Intrigued as she was by her amusing and clever new friends, she could not prevent her gaze straying frequently to the entrance, or her eyes from listening to the announcements.

Sir Constantine arrived before the first dance, inevitably with his acolyte, Mr. Clifford, in toe. He caught sight of Linnet at once. But instead of starting toward her as he usually did, he merely pressed his hand over his heart and bowed before he walked away with his handkerchief raised to his face. Mr. Clifford patted his arm and glowered at her.

Her breath caught. She wanted to laugh, with no very clear idea why. As the orchestra struck up for the first country dance, Lord Braithwaite asked Linnet to stand up with him. She accepted gracefully, trying not to feel too overwhelmed by the distinction, for she was worldly enough to know that his favor secured her success this evening. However, she discovered him to be a serious man with a twinkle in his eyes and found his company beguiling enough to distract her from constantly looking toward the entrance.

On returning to her seat, Linnet discovered Dr. Lampton had joined them with a very regal lady whom he introduced as Princess von Rheinwald.

"His betrothed," Mrs. Grant put in.

Linnet hoped she hid her surprise. Blackhaven was indeed an odd place when a country doctor was engaged to marry a princess. But perhaps the title was a nickname or a joke she didn't properly understand.

"My son and I missed all the excitement at the lake, I hear," the princess said in very faintly accented

English. "Was it not your little brother who fell through the ice, Miss James?"

"Indeed, it was. If Mr. Wolfe had not dragged him out so quickly, I dread to think of the consequences."

"Speak of the devil," Grant drawled, and Linnet's heart skipped a beat.

She glanced up and found Wolfe strolling toward their table. Dressed in correct black evening clothes with a snowy white cravat, he looked handsome and elegant. Panic surged, pleasure and pain so mixed that she couldn't tell which was which. His gaze merely brushed over her, which at least gave her time to gather her thoughts while Grant introduced him as his old friend Jack Wolfe, presenting him to the princess, to Lord and Lady Braithwaite, and to Dr. Lampton.

The doctor merely murmured, "We've met."

Somehow, space had opened up beside Linnet. She could barely breathe as Wolfe pulled up a chair and sat beside her.

"You are not dancing," he observed.

"But I have already danced with Lord Braithwaite," she managed.

"And the next dance is a waltz," Mrs. Grant remarked casually.

Wolfe smiled and turned to Linnet. "Then I hope you'll dance it with me."

"Of course, if you're brave enough," she said at once. "I have not waltzed in three years and will probably tread all over your toes."

Laughter lit his eyes, and her heart turned over with traitorous ease. "I'll take my chance," Wolfe said with mock courage. "If you will."

"Don't believe in his modesty, Miss James," Grant advised. "He dances as well as any of Wellington's officers."

She smiled, but although part of her longed to dance with him, was excited at the prospect of being held in his arms, at the same time, her anxiety doubled. Would her refusal upset him or merely hurt his pride? Could she even bring herself to give that refusal? With dread in her heart, it was difficult to maintain any part in the bantering conversation around her.

The country dance ended, its final note sounding like a knell of doom to Linnet's over-sensitive ears.

"Be brave, Miss James," Wolfe said cheerfully. "Our time has come!"

She tried to smile, hoping her nervousness would be unnoticed as everyone rose to dance—Dr. Lampton with his princess, Lord Braithwaite with Mrs. Grant, and Mr. Grant with Lady Braithwaite.

Linnet walked onto the floor with her hand just touching Wolfe's coat sleeve, so that he wouldn't feel her trembling. All the same, her heart seemed to rush when he turned and took her in his arms. He smiled reassuringly, and she tried to smile back, but he did not speak until the music began and he maneuvered her expertly through the converging couples.

"What is it?" he asked quietly. "What has upset you?"

"The pearls," she blurted, grasping at the first thing she could think of. "You should not have redeemed them."

"But they look beautiful on you." He turned her, waltzing her backward and then to the side.

"It isn't the point," she got out, trying not to be flattered that he thought so.

"But it is. I know they were your grandmother's and you were loath to part with them. It was the act of a friend."

Gathering her strength, she held his gaze. It was difficult when he was so close, his hand warm at her waist, his leg brushing against her skirts as they danced. He danced with grace and confidence, and she wished she could simply enjoy the experience. "Are we friends, Mr. Wolfe?"

She meant only that they had not known each other long enough to be true friends, but his clear, blue eyes began to smolder in a manner that gave her butterflies.

He said softly. "I hope we can be more."

She said nothing, partly because her mouth and her mind seemed to dry up, and partly because she hoped if she said nothing, he would change the subject.

He didn't. "Should I ask my question now, or shall we go somewhere private?"

"No," she managed. "Say nothing."

He blinked, and a trace of amusement entered his eyes. "Nothing at all?"

"Talk about the weather, perhaps, or—"

"Oh, dull stuff," he teased. "Please, my dear, don't look at me like that. Let us be comfortable again. Linnet, will you—"

"No," she interrupted in anguish, and his eyebrows flew up. "Please, I know what you're going to say and my answer is no. I'm so sorry. Maybe we should stop dancing now."

"Maybe we should," he agreed with enough grimness to sink her heart. And yet, he didn't stop, but weaved through the other couples with increased enthusiasm until, suddenly, she was spun into a small alcove, Wolfe jerked the curtain closed and turned to face her.

Linnet clasped her hands together, trying to control their shaking. "Please understand," she pleaded. "You have been a good friend to me, to all my family. I shall be forever grateful for the way you saved Will, and stood up to those footpads."

"And redeemed the pearls," he said, a dangerous glitter entering his eyes. "Don't forget that."

"But the pearls make it all worse," she said wildly. "You must see…it's almost as if you're *buying* me!"

His lips parted. His eyes narrowed as he stared at her. "*Buying* you? With my debts and paltry allowance? You are quite mistaken. I never pretended this would be a good bargain for you. Forgive me, I see that I was mistaken, too. Good evening."

With a small, stiff bow, he turned on his heel and went out, letting the curtain swish closed again behind him, shrouding her at last in blessed privacy.

She didn't feel blessed. She had lost him before he was even hers.

Sinking into the nearest armchair, she dropped her cheek into her hand and let the tears come.

CHAPTER NINE

ONLY SECONDS LATER, the curtain swished again, giving her no time to hide her tears from whichever stranger had blundered in. She slid her hand further over her face, hoping that if she didn't look up, whoever it was would retreat from her distress immediately. It wouldn't halt the gossip, but she couldn't make herself care.

For an instant, the intruder didn't move, and then suddenly he was crouched before her. His fingers closed around her wrist, drawing her hand away. *Wolfe.* A deep frown marred his brow.

She gasped. "Please go away, sir, this is not kind—"

"Of course I won't go away and leave you like this," he said briskly. "What is the matter? Why are you weeping?"

She waved one helpless hand while with the other, she searched desperately for the handkerchief in her reticule. He caught her hand again, pushing his own large handkerchief into it. Gratefully, she wiped her eyes.

"Why?" he asked relentlessly.

"Oh, you know why," she said brokenly, and fresh tears soaked his handkerchief. "You know perfectly well I l-love you!"

There was a pause. Appalled by her own blurted words, she risked glancing at him over the handker-chief.

He was staring at her, his frown quite vanished. "You do?"

She closed her eyes and nodded miserably.

"Then why are you set against accepting my offer?" he demanded.

A laugh that sounded more like a hiccup broke from her. "Oh, I'm not! If only you knew... But in truth, I could not tolerate such disrespect from you, or the disgrace of my family."

His eyes widened. "I know I'm not a particularly good man, but I'm not *that* bad, am I?"

"Oh, you have been so kind to us, but I can't, I truly cannot accept a carte blanche from you!"

He closed his mouth, staring at her. Slowly, a wick-ed smile began to dawn. "What on earth made you think I would offer you a carte blanche?"

"The difference in our stations, our fortunes…"

"For a clever girl," he said, "you can be a total widgeon. You should have let me speak. I want to *marry* you, not make you my mistress."

She pressed her hand to her heart. "Marry me?"

"Marry you," he repeated. "Does that change your answer?"

She swallowed and shook her head. "Not if you don't love me," she whispered. "I could not bear that. Sir, this—"

He swooped, dragging her out of the chair and across his knees. "How could I not love you, you foolish—" The rest was lost in her mouth as he kissed her as if he would never stop.

She never wanted him to stop. With a sob of joy, she flung one arm around his neck and kissed him back with relief and wonder, until his passion set fire to her own, and she lost all knowledge of her surroundings.

Fortunately, Wolfe did not. He rose to his feet with her still in his arms and, groaning, separated his mouth from hers. "Enough for now, or I'll ravish you where you stand." He set her gently back in the chair, though his avid eyes seemed reluctant to leave her lips.

She clung to his hand. "But do you really wish to be married?"

"To you," he said firmly.

"But your family, your father—"

"My father will be glad to see me settle down. My parents will both love you. And your family."

"But you, Jack? I don't think settling down is in your nature."

"To me, it isn't settling. It's fresh battles I'll fight alongside you. *For* you. I want you to be my wife, Linnet, more than I ever wanted anything, even my commission! And I'll take care of your family, too, not to buy you, just because I like them and it's the right thing to do."

She pressed his hand to her cheek. "I'm sorry I said that. I have just been so anxious as to how to answer you."

He grinned. "I suppose I should have kept my mouth shut or made the question clearer from the outset. It never entered my head you would misunderstand." He reached down, retrieving a pin and replacing it with just a little too much skill for a virtuous man. "Now, if we both look respectable enough, we might have a few minutes left of this waltz."

Half-laughing, she rose. He took her in his arms and waltzed her through the curtain and back onto the dance floor as if it was the most natural thing in the world.

"Linnet," he said. "Do you like Haughleigh House? Would you like to live near Blackhaven?"

She thought about it. "Actually, yes, I do and I would. Would you?"

"Yes," he said, as though surprised. "But I would happily live anywhere with you."

And he did.

ABOUT MARY LANCASTER

Mary Lancaster's first love was historical fiction. Her other passions include coffee, chocolate, red wine and black and white films – simultaneously where possible. She hates housework.

As a direct consequence of the first love, she studied history at St. Andrews University. She now writes full time at her seaside home in Scotland, which she shares with her husband, three children and a small, crazy dog.

Connect with Mary on-line:

Email Mary: Mary@MaryLancaster.com

Website: www.MaryLancaster.com

Newsletter sign-up: http://eepurl.com/b4Xoif

Facebook Author Page:
facebook.com/MaryLancasterNovelist

Facebook Timeline:
facebook.com/mary.lancaster.1656

Printed in Great Britain
by Amazon

38897242R00081